MOE "SNAKE EYES" JUAREZ

DETECTIVE STORIES

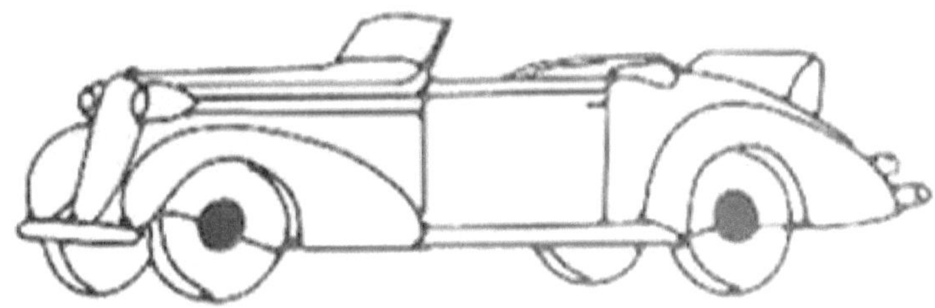

From East Los Angeles

During the 1940's

A Book Fiction by Robert Nerbovig

Cover Art by Robert Nerbovig

solartoys@yahoo.com

Prologue

The year was 1940, and the unforgiving sun beat down on the dusty streets of East Los Angeles, turning the asphalt into a shimmering mirage. Inside his cramped office, Moe "Snake-Eyes" Juarez mopped his brow with a sweat-stained handkerchief. The air hung heavy with the smell of stale cigarettes and desperation. Three years had passed since he'd traded the smoky haze of underground gambling dens for the uncertainty of private investigation, and business, to put it mildly, was slow.

Snake-Eyes hadn't exactly been a choirboy in his younger days. His arrest at a crooked casino in El Monte at the tender age of 25 was a badge of dishonor he wore with a rueful smile. But that life, a life filled with the adrenaline rush of marked cards and shady characters, had eventually soured. He craved something

more, something legitimate. So, with a past that reeked of backroom deals and whispered secrets, Snake-Eyes decided to go straight – or at least as straight as a man with his connections could manage. His tiny office, nestled above a noisy bakery on Whittier Boulevard, was a testament to his newfound (and somewhat precarious) path. The walls were adorned with cheap detective novels and faded wanted posters, the only real decoration a framed photograph of a woman with a smile as bright as the California sun. Her name was Amelia, his wife, gone too soon from a bout of the Spanish Flu. The picture served as a constant reminder of the life he was trying to build, a life where justice, not chance, determined the outcome.

Lola is Being Threatened

The smoke from Moe's cigarette hung thick in the dimly lit office. His fedora was tilted low over his eyes as he studied the black and white crime scene photos strewn across his desk. Another dead-end case involving the Eastside mob.

Just then, the door swung open and a beautiful dame sashayed in, all curves and red lipstick. Moe recognized her instantly - Lola Ramirez, a singer at one of the Cuban joints down on Brooklyn Avenue.

"Mr. Juarez," she purred, "I need your help. Someone's been leaving me threats, ugly notes shoved under my dressing room door."

Moe took a long drag on his cigarette. "Why come to me, Lola? With your connections, you know plenty of boys who could take care of this."

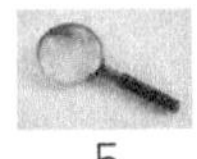

Lola's eyes flashed defiantly. "Because I want someone I can trust. Someone who plays by their own rules." She reached into her purse and slapped down a wad of cash. "What do you say, Snake-Eyes?"

He picked up the money and started counting. Whatever mess Lola was mixed up in, he was already knee-deep. "Guess I'm on the case, Lola baby. But it's gonna cost you..."

Moe folded the cash and tucked it into his coat pocket. "Don't worry your pretty little head, I'll get to the bottom of this. Where can I find you when I got a lead?"

Lola wrote down her address on a slip of paper, the Biltmore Hotel downtown. "I'm performing nightly at the Tropicana Room. Don't be a stranger, Snake-Eyes." She gave him a lingering look before turning to leave, her ruby red dress swishing against the doorframe.

After she left, Moe lit another cigarette, mulling over what little he had to go on so far. He knew Lola moved in dangerous circles - her ex-husband Enzo Castellano was a capo in the Palermo crime family. Had he picked up a new plastered pal who was looking to make Lola his own? Or were her threats coming from a jealous admirer?

There was only one way to find out. Moe grabbed his coat and fedora and headed out into the smoky East LA night. A couple blocks over, he pulled up in his Buick convertible outside a dimly lit cantina called Club Intimo. This was one of the joints where Lola used to croon before she hit the big time.

The jukebox was playin' a smokey bolero tune as Snake-Eyes sidled up to the bar. "Dos cervezas, Eduardo," he said, slapping a quarter on the battered wood.

The bartender's eyes widened as he recognized Moe. "Juarez, I heard you was out of the game, compadre. What brings a P.I. like you around these parts again?"
Moe slid one of the cervezas towards Eduardo. "I'm working, Eddie. Need to learn what you know about who might be leanin' on Lola Ramirez."
Eddie lifted the bottle to his lips, taking a slow pull. "Lola...now there's a name I ain't heard in a long time. That little senorita used to shake her moneymaker something fierce on my stage before the big leagues came callin'."
"So you heard from her recently? Anyone hassling her, maybe an old flame with a jealous streak?" Moe pressed.
Shaking his head, Eddie replied, "You know I can't be breakin' confidences, Moe. But those Eastside barzones? They got a mean possessive streak when it comes to their working girls..."

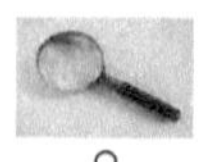

Moe nodded slowly, a pit forming in his gut. He knew Eddie was referring to the notorious gang that ran rackets throughout East LA. If they had their sights set on Lola, she could be in real danger.

"Gracias, Eddie. You've given me enough to go on." Moe tossed back the last of his cerveza and slapped a couple more quarters on the bar. As he turned to leave, a loud crash came from the back room followed by raised voices.

Acting on instinct honed from years on the streets, Moe pulled his .38 special from his shoulder holster and crept towards the commotion. He could make out at least three men arguing in Spanish, their tones getting more and more heated. Moe burst through the door his gun raised. "Alright cabrones, keep your hands where I can see them!"

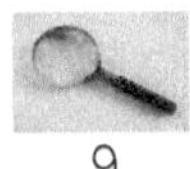

The two larger men had gravely expressions and snake tattoos on their necks - definite Eastside barzones. But it was the slight man cowering in the corner that caught Moe's eye. He recognized that weaselly face from the crime scene photos - Enzo Castellano's Capo, Miguel "El Raton" Quesada.

"Well, well, if it ain't Snake-Eyes Juarez," the taller barzone sneered. "You still slingin' that peashooter and pretendin' to be a detective?"

Before Moe could respond, El Raton raised his hands shakily. "He's telling the truth, Julio! I've heard of this Juarez...he ain't afraid to go too far."

"Can it, Raton," Julio growled. "We're takin' you back to Don Castellano. And as for you, Juarez..." His hand moved towards his jacket, no doubt going for the shotgun he had stashed.

That's when all hell broke loose. Moe's .38 thundered as he dropped Julio with two quick shots to the chest. The other barzone reached for his piece, but Moe was quicker on the trigger, punching three holes right through the snake tat on his neck. He went down without a sound.

El Raton was still sniveling in the corner when Moe grabbed him by the lapels and slammed him against the wall. "Start talking, Raton! What's your play with Lola and I'll make sure you get to see Don Castellano again..."

El Raton's eyes were wide with terror as Moe's revolver pressed against his doughy cheek. "Okay, okay! I'll spill!" he squealed.

"Lola left Don Castellano for that singer Puente last year. The Don didn't take it well. He put a hit out on the two lovebirds," El Raton babbled. "But they

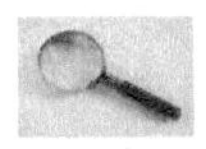

got wind of it and split town before we could collect."

Moe tightened his grip, letting the pistol dig in a little deeper. "If that's true, then why circle back now? Why start leaving Lola threats after all this time?"

The little capo started trembling harder. "I d-don't know, I swear! The Don's been obsessed, thinking Lola was playing him for a sucker! He wanted to flush her out into the open, get her scared enough to show herself. That's all I know I swear on mi Madre!"

Snake-Eyes studied the weasel's face, deciding he was telling the truth. He holstered his .38 and gave El Raton a hard shove back against the wall. "You just bought yourself a chance, Raton. But you tell Castellano, if he even thinks about going near Lola again, there'll be more holes comin' to him next time."

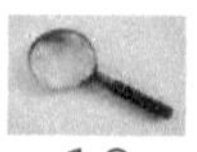

Leaving the cowering capo behind, Moe hurried out to his car, tires squealing as he raced towards downtown. If what El Raton said was true, the whole situation with Lola was even more twisted than he thought. Don Castellano wanting revenge on his ex-wife years later? And someone using those threats to try and draw her out?

This whole thing reeked of a pit of lies that someone was waiting at the bottom of. As Moe's Buick ate up the miles towards the Biltmore, he racked his brain, trying to put the scattered pieces together. One thing was clear - if he didn't get to Lola soon, that pit was liable to swallow them both whole. As Moe's Buick growled to a stop outside the Biltmore Hotel, he quickly scanned the elegant entrance and the crowded valet area. So far, no obvious signs of trouble. He ducked inside and made his

way through the opulent lobby towards the Tropicana Room.

The smoky lounge was packed with high-rollers and Diamond Dolls circulating with trays of cocktails. On the small stage, a Latin big band was laying down a brassy, swinging rhythm. And there, draped elegantly over a barstool microphone, was Lola in a shimmering red dress that left little to the imagination.

Her eyes found Moe's as she sang the final, yearning notes of "Besame Mucho." A barely perceptible nod told him she'd noticed his arrival. Lola purred, "Why don't you cowboys let the new band take over?

As Lola slinked off the stage, Moe pushed through the crowd towards her. Up close, he could see the worried lines around her eyes, offsetting that celebrated beauty.

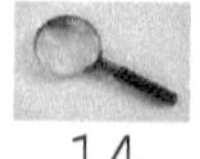

"We need to talk, hermosa. In private,"
he muttered.

Lola nodded curtly and led him into a
back hallway, away from the lounge's
prying eyes and ears. "What is it? Did
you find out who's been leaving those
notes?"

"Maybe," Moe replied, lighting a fresh
cigarette to buy some time. "The way I
understand it, Don Castellano is still
carrying a big-time grudge towards you
over walking out. Put a hit out at one
point, aiming to put you and that singer
Puente down for good."

Lola's perfectly rouged lips parted in
surprise. "Enzo? But that was over a year
ago! Why would he come after me now?"

Moe shrugged. "From what I could get out
of his capo, the Don's still carrying a
mean obsession with you, mami. Convinced
you played him. The threats were his way

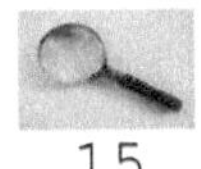

15

of trying to smoke you out into the open again."

"Dios mio..." Lola sank back against the wall, a trembling hand going to her corseted waist. "Moe, you have to believe me - I never wanted any of this! I was just trying to escape that life of violence."

Snake-Eyes took a long pull on his cigarette, considering. "I believe you, Lola. But we're still missin' some big pieces here. Someone else is pullin' the strings behind these threats, aimin' to set you and your ex against each other for good."

Just then, a sharp whistle came from the other end of the hallway. They both turned to see the beefy form of Johnny Puente, the singer Lola had run off with, leveling a .45 automatic at them with outrageous calm.

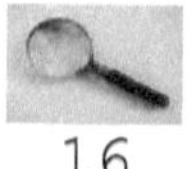

"Should've known better than to keep snoopin', Juarez," Puente sneered. "This has been a long time coming for me and my Lolita." He swung the pistol towards the stunned woman. "I am sorry, mamacita, but you left me no choice..."
Moe tensed, his hand inching towards the .38 under his coat. But Puente's .45 was already trained squarely on Lola. "I wouldn't try it, detective. You'll just get this beautiful señorita killed faster."
"Johnny, what are you doing?" Lola's voice was plaintive, betrayed. "After everything we've been through, how could you do this to me?"
The Cuban singer's face contorted with rage. "To you? You stuck-up bitch, you did this to me! Stringing me along with sweet nothings about leaving the vida loca behind." He took a step closer, the gun unwavering. "All so you could bleed

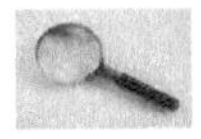

17

me dry and crawl back to that mafioso husband of yours!"

Realization crashed over Moe like a wave. The truth they'd been missing finally became clear. "So that's the name of that tune, huh Puente? All this violence, all because Lola finally wised up and decided to ditch your narcissistic hide."

Puente rounded on him, spittle flying. "Can it, Juarez! I got permission from the biggest narco hoods in the city to take her out. Just needed to make her big shot ex think she was playin' him again first." His face split into an ugly grin. "Kinda like shooting two birds with one shot, if you know what I mean."

The Cuban's finger tightened on the trigger inexorably. But just before he could squeeze off a shot, Moe moved with Snake-Eyes speed. He ripped the pistol from his shoulder holster and opened

fire, the thundering report of his .38
echoing like doom in the tight hallway.
Puente barely had time for his eyes to
widen before the heavy slugs slammed into
his chest, flinging him backwards like a
rag doll. His arms flew out to the sides
as he crumpled, the big .45 automatic
clattering uselessly to the tile floor.
Moe rushed to Lola's side, gripping her
bare shoulders firmly as she stared at
her former lover's lifeless form. "You
okay, mamacita? That scheming yucca got
what he had comin'."
She nodded wordlessly, throwing her arms
around Moe's neck as she broke down
crying into his shoulder. "Gracias, you
are my guardian angel. I don't know how
I'll ever repay you..."
Holding her shuddering frame close, Moe
pressed his whiskered cheek to Lola's
silken waves of dark hair and sighed.
"Hey, don't mention it, hermosa. A guy

could get used to playing the hero now and again..."

Two weeks later

Moe flicked away his spent cigarette butt as he strolled out of the Mission District courthouse, tugging his battered fedora low against the bright California sun. Another successful day defending the dime bag hoods and barrio lowlifes that helped keep his cheap office afloat.

As he crossed the street towards his Buick coupe, a sleek black Cadillac convertible purred up alongside the curb. Moe's hand went instinctively for his shoulder holster before he recognized the driver - Lola, looking as radiant as ever in a white sundress and oversized shades. "Get in, Snake-Eyes," she called with a dazzling smile. "I'm taking you out for a celebratory lunch. My treat for once."

He raised an eyebrow but didn't need to be asked twice. Swinging his lanky frame over the door and into the buttery leather passenger seat, Moe couldn't help grinning back at her. "If this is how you treat all your friends, I might just get into trouble more often."

Lola laughed, that rich warm sound that always tied Moe's belly in knots. As the powerful Caddy accelerated smoothly away from the curb, she slid her hand over to give his rough knuckles an affectionate squeeze.

"You've done enough noble deeds to last a lifetime, mi Angel. From now on, just think of me as your own personal chaperone..." Her ruby lips curled in a smile filled with promise. "...away from trouble."

Chuckling deep in his throat, Moe laced his fingers through Lola's and raised them to his whiskered cheek with

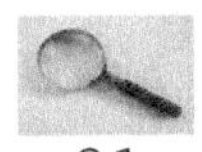

21

undisguised tenderness. For once, his sights weren't on the next shady case or crooked racket around the next barrio corner.

He was too busy picturing a whole new kind of adventure, one where the dashing detective and the sultry songbird rode off into the California sunset together. If that meant playing the hero for his gorgeous partner, well, Snake-Eyes was calling that an even trade.

Lupe is Missing

In the months that followed, Moe "Snake-Eyes" Juarez's caseload only grew more varied and complex - he found a priceless Mayan artifact traded on the black market, trailed an actor's wandering eyes and camera to his mistress's apartment, and even helped solve a grisly murder outside of a downtown diner. No matter how high or low the client, Moe could

always be counted on to snake out the truth.

The cases kept rolling in for Moe "Snake-Eyes" Juarez over the years. A knock at the door revealed an anxious young man named Tommy Salazar who came into Moe's office wringing his flat cap in his hands.

"I need you to find my sister, Lupe," Tommy said, his voice cracking. "She's been missing for three days."

Moe leaned back in his creaky desk chair. "Tell me more about this sister of yours."

"She's 19 years old, works as a waitress over at Millie's Diner on 7th Street. Last anyone saw of her she was leaving work after her night shift Tuesday evening." Tommy's eyes were wet with unshed tears. "Please Mr. Juarez, you gotta help me. Lupe's all I got left in this world."

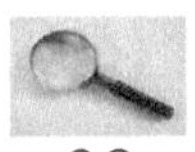

23

Moe gave the young man a reassuring nod. "Don't worry kid, I'll do everything I can to track down your sister."

He started his investigation over at Millie's Diner, questioning Lupe's coworkers and the patrons who were there the night she disappeared. One creepy-looking lineman with a moustache waxed too perfectly admitted to slipping Lupe a note with his number after she brought him his check. Moe's neck grew hot watching the guy describe the chase he clearly had planned.

The next step was to retrace Lupe's usual walking route home from the diner. On the third day, Moe came across some troubling details - some shredded fabric from a woman's shirt and smears of blood on the ground near a back alley. He bagged it to get analyzed by his contact down at the crime lab.

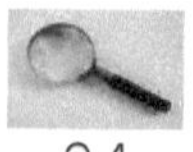

By following the trail of evidence, Moe finally traced Lupe's whereabouts to none other than the deviant lineman's apartment. He turned the evidence over to the police, who surrounded the apartment and arrested the sicko inside. Lupe was freed, scared but alive, thank God.

Moe's heart swelled see the many tears of joy on Tommy's face when he returned his little sister to him. "How can I ever repay you, Mr. Juarez?" the young man asked, hugging Lupe tightly.

Moe just shook his head and tipped his fedora. "No need, kid. Just doing my job."

Cases like Lupe Salazar's were the ones that made the long hours and gritty work worthwhile for Moe. But there were plenty of other seedy jobs that came across his desk too.

Newborn Discovery

It all came to a head one blistering night in July. Moe was staking out an Auto World factory downtown, trying to catch employees making drops with a local bookie ring. He was hunkered down in his Buick, a cold sweat making his undershirt cling, when he heard a gut-churning sound - a baby's cries.

Moe froze, the noise like a siren cutting through the thick night air. It was coming from the Auto World lot, near the east entrance. He crept from his car and followed the cries, his heart pounding. There, wrapped in a soiled blanket and tucked beside a dumpster, was a newborn infant girl. Her face was blistered and raw from the searing summer heat. Moe snatched her up, her wails of misery making his soul clench. Who could be so heartless as to abandon a child like this?

His stakeout instantly forgotten, Moe raced to the emergency room downtown, still cradling the screaming baby against his chest. "She needs help!" he shouted as nurses came rushing over. "Found her in an alley by the Auto World plant."

In the wake of that shattering experience, Moe found he could no longer stomach the darker side of his PI work. He gave up taking posing jobs and instead chose casework that only involved factual investigations, inheritance disputes, that sort of thing. The horrors he'd seen made his soul feel too hollow inside.

He didn't have the energy to pursue the mystery of who'd dumped that poor infant. But Moe developed a restless obsession with the baby's ultimate fate, making discreet inquiries to nurses for months after. Finally, he learned she'd been taken into foster care and later adopted by a loving family. The thought of that

little fighter getting a second chance was one of the few reprieves from the darkness that kept Moe going.

The months marched on, each one seeming to pass quicker than the last for Moe "Snake-Eyes" Juarez. Case after case blurred together - accusing spouses, shady business dealings, every seedier side of human nature he was constantly hired to expose. The baby he'd rescued never left Moe's mind, a tiny beacon of light amongst the shadows.

Separating the Diamonds

His next case was a wealthy jeweler named Hector Rodrigo came into Moe's shoebox office, his face flushed and sweating despite the desert cooler whirring away. "You gotta help me, Juarez," Rodrigo panted, loosening his silk tie. "I've been getting threats, letters saying

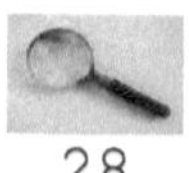

terrible things will happen if I don't pay up."

"Sounds like a nice little extortion racket," Moe said, already able to smell the greenbacks. "You got any ideas who might be leaning on you, Mr. Rodrigo?"

The jeweler's eyes flitted around nervously. "I didn't want to go to the cops because...well, I've been stepping out on my wife, if you know what I mean. With a few different mistresses. I'm afraid one of their jealous husbands could be behind these threats."

Moe sighed and lit a cigarette. Just another day walking the line between doing his job and keeping shady businesses quiet. "Don't worry, my lips are sealed. Why don't you start by telling me about these dames you've been seeing on the side?"

Over the next few weeks, Moe did some careful recon, tracking down and tailing

each of Rodrigo's mistresses and their husbands. He didn't find any concrete leads on the extortion threats. But he did spot the jeweler's wife Carmen following her husband one night, catching him stepping out of a cheap motel room with his arms around a redheaded bombshell.

When Moe updated Rodrigo with this twist, the jeweler turned white as a sheet. "Carmen knows? Oh my God, she's going to take me for everything! You have to help me get ahead of this, Juarez!"

So, in a discreet meeting, Moe served up all the evidence he'd gathered of Rodrigo's infidelities - greasy burger wrappers, hotel receipts with dodgy crossed-out names, the whole unsavory pie. He pushed it across the desk to a red-faced but steadfast Carmen.

"The way I see it, ma'am, you've got all the leverage you need for one hell of a generous divorce settlement," Moe said. Carmen stared at the pile for a long moment, then swept it all into her purse without a word. On her way out, she paused and tucked a neat stack of bills onto Moe's desk - double his initial fee. "Gracias, Mr. Juarez. For handing me back the truth, no matter how ugly," she said. Her jaw was set, her court seemingly ruled.

Dona and the IRS

Cases like this were all too common in those first few years as Moe established his reputation around East LA. He tailed cheating spouses, did basic nightclub stakeouts, whatever seedy allegations folks could raise enough cash to have investigated. Moe tried to zone out the moral side of it, just focused on

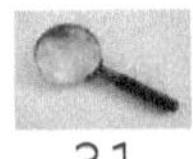

following the trail wherever it led. He knew this was just him paying his dues on the dust-bitten road to bigger and more sophisticated cases.

One of those arrived when Moe was hired by an unlikely client - the Italian widow Doña Costanza, one of the wealthiest women in East LA. Her husband Cesar had died tragically a few years earlier when their mansion burned down, taking him and most of their valuables with it. Now the grief-stricken Doña was being reamed by the IRS over the estate taxes.

"The crooks at internal revenue don't believe all my claims about the fine arts and jewels lost in that horrible fire," she told Moe in her thick accent. "They think I'm lying to avoid the taxes on all those treasures!"

"So, you need me to try and dig up some evidence substantiating what got torched

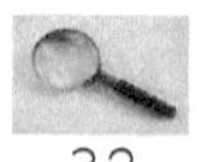

that night?" Moe asked, already able to smell the fat payday.

"Si, si, whatever you can find!" Doña nodded frantically. "I'm telling the truth every precious belonging went up in the fire when my dear Cesar..." She dissolved into fresh sobs.

Over the next few weeks, Moe turned over every possible rock around the tragic mansion fire from several years earlier. He tracked down the first responders, neighbors who witnessed the blaze, and even a shady former servant of the Costanza family who'd been fired just days before the fateful night.

Slowly, Moe pieced together a shocking possibility - that the deadly fire may in fact have been started deliberately. And when he shared his theory with Doña Costanza, the grief-stricken widow collapsed into a haunted silence.

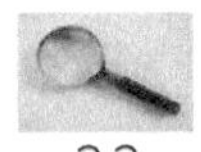

The faded blue eyes of Doña Costanza were round with dismay as Moe laid out his findings. "Deliberately, you mean arson?" she whispered, clutching the lace shawl tighter around her slender shoulders.

Moe nodded grimly. "I've tracked down enough little threads to make me believe your husband's death that night wasn't just a tragic accident, Doña. I think someone set that fire intentionally."

The elderly widow's face crumpled as she absorbed this gut-wrenching revelation. After several moments, she lifted her chin, a hardness returning to her aristocratic features. "Tell me everything, Mr. Juarez. I must know the full truth."

And so Moe recounted all the pieces of evidence he'd unearthed - the fired servant who'd been overheard issuing threats against the Costanza family, the

traces of accelerant found in the ashes of the grand foyer where the inferno had started, and most crucially, newly analyzed fingerprints from the crime scene that didn't match anyone in the household.

"This wasn't just a random act of violence though," Moe said, spreading the damning fingerprint cards out on the desk. "These prints belong to a small-time arsonist I've dealt with before - a real sicko who sells his services to the highest bidder looking to commit insurance fraud."

Doña Costanza stared at the evidence, silent tears tracking down her papery cheeks. "All this time...I have mourned my beloved as an innocent victim. But poor Cesar...he was murdered, wasn't he?" Her voice broke on the final words.

Moe averted his eyes, uncomfortable being the bearer of such profoundly ugly truth

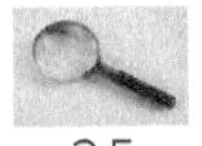

to this sweet old soul. But it was his job to lay out the facts as he found them.

"I'm so sorry, Doña. By all the evidence, it does appear your husband was killed - sacrificed to whoever hired that arsonist as part of an elaborate insurance swindle."

In the heavy silence that followed, Moe didn't quite know what else to say. He could still hear the rapid flutter of Doña's breath, the soft weeping she tried but failed to stifle. Just when he thought she might keel over from shock, she sat up straight once more.

"Thank you, Mr. Juarez," she said with surprising strength. "Thank you for finally tearing the veil off this terrible crime against my family. I always knew in my heart there were vultures circling my Cesar's great fortune, hoping for just such an opportunity to strike."

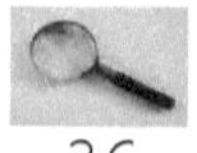

She reached into the folds of her dress
and retrieved a small velvet bag, sliding
it across the desk to Moe. It was heavy,
clinking like coins. "For your integrity,
Mr. Juarez. And for never giving up on
uncovering the truth."

Moe held the small fortune in his
calloused hand, his throat tightening. "I
didn't do it for any reward, Doña. Just
wanted to learn what really happened that
awful night." He tried giving her a
reassuring smile. "Now you've got to be
strong, ma'am. The police can finally
have a straight run at the monsters
behind this."

And true to her resilient nature, Doña
Costanza squared her shoulders and nodded
firmly. "Si, you're right. It's time to
do whatever is necessary to avenge my
Cesar." She fixed Moe with a determined
gaze. "Will you stay on and consult for
the investigators, Mr. Juarez? I could

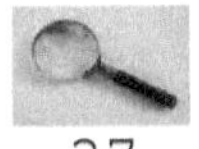

use your clear eye to guide me through the storm ahead."

Moe knew he shouldn't get even deeper involved in such a high-profile case, and certainly one haunted by the specter of deadly arson. But looking into the proud, bereaved eyes of this steel-willed matriarch, he couldn't find it in him to refuse.

"You've got it, Doña," he said with a nod. "I'm with you until we get to the bottom of this bad business, no matter how far down the rabbit hole it goes."

Over the course of the next few months, the dogged investigation into the Costanza fire uncovered a sordid web of greed and deceit by a shadowy cabal of local businessmen and crime syndicates. They had indeed conspired to have the wealthy Don Costanza murdered in an elaborate insurance fraud scheme, hoping

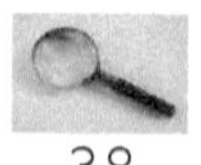

to plunder his family's fortune in the aftermath.

It took several mistrials, but eventually Moe's evidence helped put three of the key arsonist conspirators behind bars. The crooks sang like canaries, revealing the names of their rich and corrupt employers who had funded the murderous plot. By 1943, nearly a dozen powerful local figures had been imprisoned as well, their shady reputations and fortunes in utter ruin.

For Doña Costanza, it was the justice she'd sought, even if it could never fill the heartbreaking void left by Cesar's death. On the day the last wealthy criminal was sentenced, she took Moe's hand in her soft, papery one.

"Gracias, Mr. Juarez," she said simply. "My beloved has finally found peace because of you."

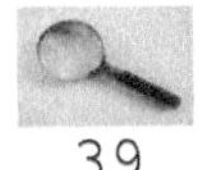

As he looked back on that letter case months later, Moe realized it was the one that truly set him on the grit-tested road from shady affair-tracker to a PI who helped put away dangerous arsonists and mobsters. It was the definitive fork in the road where he chose the path his moral coded heartbeat wanted him to follow, even if it meant walking squarely into the darkest of this city's criminal underbellies.

With the Costanza arson case providing his first big takedown of powerful criminal players, Moe "Snake-Eyes" Juarez found his reputation around East LA shifting in a new direction. Whereas he'd once been just another downtrodden private dick trailing cheating spouses, now some of the city's biggest movers and shakers sought out his tenacious investigation skills.

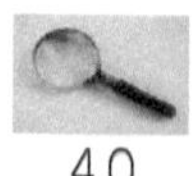

Family Property Holdout

One such lucrative opportunity came knocking when a high-powered attorney named Phillip Graves arrived at Moe's dingy office. Graves was representing a group of wealthy businessmen looking to develop a swath of land out in the dusty hills north of the city. The only snag - a stubborn property owner named Hector Ramos refused to sell the choice acres his family had owned for generations.

"Mr. Ramos claims he's received threats, warning him to vacate his property or face violent consequences," Graves said, laying a fat envelope of bills on Moe's desk. "My clients want you to prove whether these threats are legitimate or just a ploy for holdings out for more money."

Moe shuffled through the generous stack of hundreds, letting out a low whistle. "I'm on the case, Mr. Graves. Your

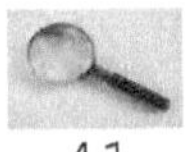

clients can count on me sniffing out the truth."

Over the next few weeks, Moe did his standard reconnaissance work - setting up sporadic stakeouts at the Ramos property, tailing the old ranch owner's every move, searching for any leads on who might want to intimidate him off his valuable land. He uncovered no concrete evidence of threats more serious than the occasional crank phone call or dead animal left on Ramos' porch as a dark prank.

Moe was starting to think the holdout rancher was batting away at shadows to try milking the property developers for a higher payout. That was, until one scorching afternoon out on the dusty Ramos acreage forever altered the trajectory of the case.

Moe was hunkered down in his sweltering car just within view of the Ramos ranch house, squinting against the shimmering

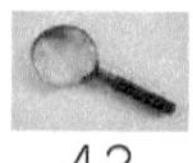

waves of heat. That's when a beat-up truck came roaring out of nowhere, speeding towards the house's rear entrance like a missile.

Three men in kerchiefs spilled from the truck's cab, all brandishing pistols. Moe's pulse spiked as he realized with cold clarity what he was witnessing - these were no idle threats, but a serious hit to terrorize the Ramos family into evacuating.

Without a second thought, Moe peeled out from his hiding spot, his Buick's tires kicking up clouds of burnt sienna dust. As the truck idled by the house, Moe brought his car careening straight towards it, striking the rear fender with a bone-jarring crunch of metal. From there, all hell broke loose.

The three gunmen whirled around, momentarily dazed before raising their weapons towards Moe with feral snarls.

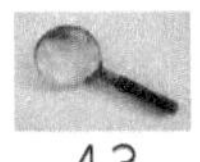

Knowing he was outgunned, Moe threw his car into reverse and hauled ass back the way he'd come, the piercing crack of bullets pinging off his trunk.

In the rearview mirror, he saw the ranch house door flinging open - an elderly Hector Ramos rushing out, shotgun in hand, his wife and teenage son on his heels. Moe kept his foot mashed on the gas as more gunfire echoed in the shimmering heat behind him.

Despite the rancher's own return volleys, one of the gunmen managed to wing Ramos in the leg before they fled back to their truck and tore off in a spray of dust and gravel. When Moe finally skidded to a stop, his heart was thundering like a snare drum in his ears.

He raced back to the ranch, shoes crunching in the dirt, to find Ramos lying in a growing pool of his own blood. His wife and son hovered over him, their

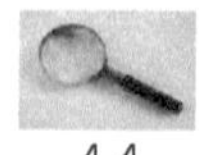

anguished shouts echoing across the valley.

"Get an ambulance here, quick! That cut on his leg went straight to the bone!" Moe yelled. He yanked off his sweaty undershirt and used it to tie off a tourniquet above the wound, trying to stop the bleeding as best he could.

"You were right about the threats, Mr. Juarez," Ramos gasped through gritted teeth, his face stamped with agony. "They want this land...bad as can be..."

While waiting for help to arrive, Moe pieced together what he could from the chaotic scene. Triangulating the tire tracks and spent bullet casings, it appeared the gunmen were aiming to scare the Ramos family into abandoning their property - but when the old rancher came outside with his shotgun, one of them lashed out in panic and shot him.

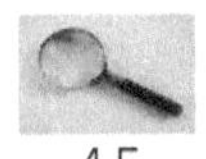

Graves' property developers had played dirtier than Moe could've imagined, actually hiring goons to terrorize the holdout landowner through violence. Though he'd arrived just in time to witness their vile tactics, Moe still felt a sharp pang of guilt that he hadn't cracked the larger extortion plot sooner before bloodshed occurred.

As the wailing ambulance arrived and EMTs rushed to stabilize Ramos, Moe pulled Phillip Graves aside and got right to the ugly point. "Your clients tried to have this family killed to make their property grab easier. I saw the whole damn thing go down myself."

To Graves' credit, the slick attorney looked briefly shaken before his professional mask reset. "Well...that's certainly a serious allegation, Juarez. Do you have any proof to back up such an incendiary claim?"

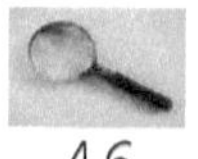

Moe almost growled in frustration. Of course the high-priced legal weasel was going to play dumb and make him work for extracting a confession. So, over the next several tense days, Moe meticulously documented every scrap of evidence he could gather - the spent bullet casings, matching them to the guns used; the property deed records showing the parcel's value; and most crucially, tracking down the identities of those three gunmen.

When Moe finally strode into Phillip Graves' downtown office with his thick file of damning evidence weeks later, the arrogant lawyer's face drained of color. Because sitting across from him were not just the well-heeled group of developers he represented, but several high-ranking detectives from the LAPD as well.

"Mr. Graves, I'll ask you one final time," Moe said, his voice low and

controlled. "Did you or any of your clients orchestrate that violent attack on Hector Ramos' family with the intent of running them off their property through violent means?"

The tense silence stretching out told Moe all he needed to know. Graves and his cohorts realized they were caught dead to rights, that no elite legal wrangling could make this go away after such a brazen act of violence. One by one, the wealthy men at the table slumped in resignation.

Moe's investigative work helped secure guilty pleas and lengthy prison sentences for Graves and three of his clients in connection with the conspiracy to threaten and harm the Ramos clan. The rest were heavily fined and forced into federal monitoring of all their business dealings going forward.

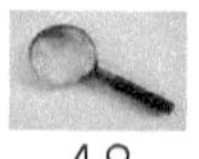

Hector Ramos, meanwhile, kept his family's precious acreage thanks to Moe's perseverance. He made a full recovery from his gunshot wound, even dropping by Moe's office one day to give his gruff thanks.

"You did good by us, Juarez. Real good," the leathery old-timer said, slapping a firm hand on Moe's shoulder. "Wouldn't have survived those pendejos trying to bully me out without you."

As the humble rancher turned to leave, Moe felt a swelling of purpose he hadn't experienced since those first rushes of adrenaline from staring down lawbreakers as a young PI. For once, his PI work had protected the vulnerable from predation by greed-choked men of power. His soul felt lighter knowing he'd helped preserve justice, even in this dusty, hard-baked corner of the world.

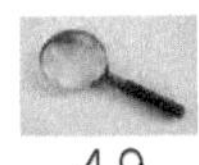

It was the kind of clarity that would help guide the tougher cases to come - the ability to lock onto doing what was righteous and moral, no matter how tangled up or intimidating the opposition. If Moe "Snake-Eyes" Juarez could keep staring down evil from that clear-eyed vantage point, he figured there was no pit of darkness he couldn't hire out to shed some light into.

The Ramos property extortion case marked a major turning point for Moe "Snake-Eyes" Juarez - no longer was he just a seedy gumshoe trailing cheating spouses and exposing tawdry affairs. Now he'd proven himself as a relentless investigator capable of taking down powerful criminal conspiracies and moneyed interests. His phone began ringing with a higher caliber of cases from the city's elite.

Large Bank Embezzlement

One such opportunity came knocking in the spring of 1944, when a dignified-looking gentleman arrived at Moe's cramped office uninvited. He introduced himself as Edgar Coleman, head of security for the esteemed California Reserve Bank downtown.

"We have an internal issue that requires your...utmost discretion, Mr. Juarez," Coleman said, passing a plain envelope across the desk. Inside was a typed letter detailing allegations of embezzlement and fund skimming occurring within the ranks of the Reserve Bank itself.

Moe frowned as he scanned the unsettling contents. "You've got a mole inside ripping you off? And you need me to get to the bottom of it while keeping things in-house?"

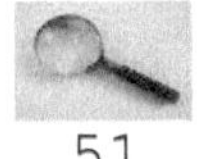

Coleman gave a terse nod. "Precisely. As a external investigator, you'll be able to delve into matters unseen while avoiding any unpleasant...public dishonor for the institution. Money is no object - we simply must neutralize this threat by any means necessary."

"You've got a deal," Moe said, sizing up the respected banker. "No financial rats will be leaving any holes un-sniffed on my watch."

And with that, he was headed undercover into the inner sanctum of the city's most prominent bank. Over the next couple of weeks, Moe ingratiated himself as a new hired security guard, blending in with the Reserve's team while discreetly poking around for any leads.

He studied records of cash transports, change orders, even the petty cash drawer sign-in logs - anything that could offer clues about who was bleeding the vault

and by what means. Moe started piecing together a likely suspect - a fresh-faced junior teller who'd recently taken a few questionable sick days right after a couple large-dollar deposits had gone briefly unaccounted for.

The young man's name was Larry Reese, a relatively new hire who'd been struggling with debts and a nasty gambling habit, according to Moe's background check. He figured Reese had probably gotten in too deep with the wrong sort of crowd and was now hemorrhaging the Reserve's funds to cover his escalating markers.

To confirm his suspicions, Moe decided to put a tail on Reese and see where he was slinking off to away from the bank. He tracked the reedy teller's movements during his off hours for several days until hitting pay dirt - camera evidence of Reese leaving a downtown pool hall through the back entrance, clutching a

thick envelope of what was unmistakably
cash.

Mole in a hole, time for Moe to spring
the trap. He arranged for Coleman and a
couple of his reserve guards to lie in
wait in that dingy back alley the
following night. When Reese emerged from
his shady porthole once again, envelope
overflowing, the pit pull was smoothly
applied.

In a matter of seconds, Coleman's men had
Reese pinned against the grungy wall, the
damning cash fluttering from the split
envelope and cascading around their feet
like oversized confetti.

"Where'd all this money come from,
Larry?" Moe asked, leveling his best
intimidating stare at the squirming
teller. "Maybe we should call the police
over and see what they think about you
walking around with god knows how many
missing Reserve Bank notes."

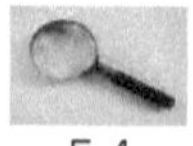

That was all it took for the cocky young man to crack, his desperate situation shattering the thin veneer of criminal bravado. Reese started sobbing right there in the alley, admitting everything - how he'd been siphoning off small increments from daily deposits and shipments, replacing the cash with dummy bundles. All of it was to pay off members of a local dice outfit who'd worked Reese over good when he couldn't cover his losses.

Over the next few days, Coleman's team was able to use Reese's panicked disclosures to recover nearly all the missing funds and cut off the reserve worm's debt-fueled pipeline. The corrupt teller got shipped off to face serious federal charges, while Coleman made good on his promise to keep the banks shady inner-workings from going public.

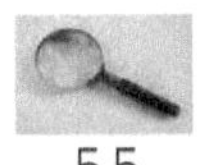

After settling the matter quietly and
discreetly, the head of Reserve security
summoned Moe back to his office and
handed him a plain envelope - packed to
the bursting with an exceedingly generous
payout.

"A bargain at ten times the price to keep
the Reserve's integrity uncompromised,"
Coleman told Moe with the faintest hint
of a smile. "You've averted a major
calamity, Mr. Juarez. I suspect your
services will be most coveted by my
counterparts at the city's other
financial institutions now."

Those words proved prophetic, as Moe's
elite career ascension continued
unabated after solving the Reserve caper.
Over time he was retained by virtually
every major bank, credit union, even the
City Treasurer's office to troubleshoot
internal malfeasance and fraud.

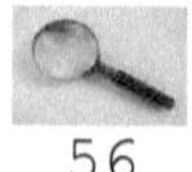

Slowly but surely, he cultivated an unimpeachable reputation as the go-to fixer capable of routing out white-collar criminals and safeguarding institutional reputations. All without the self-serving hunger for glory or public plaudits that corrupted so many in his field.

Though Moe "Snake-Eyes" Juarez had climbed to the upper echelons of East LA's private investigation scene, he knew better than to rest on his prestigious laurels. The darkness and corruption that festered in this city's concrete arteries had an insidious way of spreading, even inching up towards the highest plateaus.

Transit Authority Bid-Rigging

He got a harsh reminder of that ugly truth when he received a coded message instructing him to make a clandestine rendezvous at a nondescript downtown

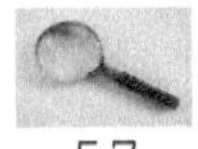

diner. His shadowy summoner was none other than James Woodson - a gruff, powerful man who headed up the city's Transit Authorities Commission.

"We've got a serious problem that needs your particular brand of discretion, Juarez," Woodson said, pushing a thick manila envelope across the Formica table. Inside were damning documents indicating a massive kickback and bid-rigging scheme being run from within the Transit Commission itself.

Moe's eyes went wide as he scanned the paperwork detailing how tens of millions of dollars in public contracts had been systematically steered towards a shadowy cabal of favored construction firms. All greased by brazen cash bribes paid through covert channels to corrupt Commission members.

"This racket has been going on for years now, getting worse every cycle as more

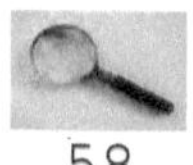

honest officials get bought off or removed," Woodson growled. "We need an outsider like you to dig in without stakes in the game and smoke out who's turning the entire TAC into their personal slush fund."

Moe frowned, realizing the cold reality - no matter how high up he climbed, the stinking rot of civic graft never stopped trying to spread its tendrils. He gave Woodson a resolute nod. "Don't worry, I'm your man to start cutting out all the cancers, no matter who or what they've infected."

And with that, Moe dove headfirst into one of the most Byzantine puzzles of municipality corruption he'd ever encountered. He burrowed into the Transit Commission's records and logs, assembling an ever-expanding web of frontmen, shell companies, and under-the-table kickbacks used to illegally

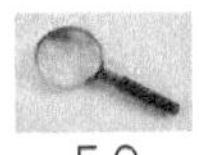

line the pockets of those awarding construction contracts.

His big break came a few months into the investigation, when Moe matched up paperwork from a small-time demolition company that had suspiciously been awarded multiple astonishingly lucrative jobs tearing down old infrastructure across the city. Deep in their invoices, Moe found a repeating account number that traced back to the personal checking account of a senior Transit Commission official.

From there, he was able to connect a handful of other similarly egregious contract overpays and suspicious awards that all tracked back financially to just three TAC commissioners. The damning money trails led all the way up to monthly payoffs being personally collected by those men from shady construction bosses around the city.

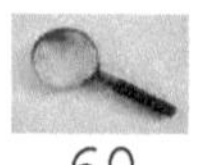

When Moe finally compiled all his comprehensive evidence dossiers, he knew he was sentencing those officials and their collaborators to potential life prison sentences if the DA's office took the case. But he also understood that Jim Woodson's desire for discretion - avoiding a massively destabilizing public scandal that could cripple the city's whole transit infrastructure.

With that need for pragmatism in mind, Moe laid it all out in Woodson's office one tension-thick afternoon. The hardcase Commissioner gave a bemused snort as he pawed through the reams of paperwork.

"I had my suspicions about Horace and those other two grease balls pretty much from day one," he said, referring to the pay-off ringleaders by name. "But having all their filthy tracks laid out in the

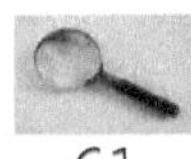

open like this now we can burn the whole rat's nest to the damned ground."

Woodson fixed Moe with an intensely studious gaze. "So, here's the play, Juarez. We blitz those three pricks anonymously with all your evidence files. Give them a chance to resign and pay back every cent they stole or we go scorched earth and end their miserable careers in disgrace before the courts and papers get involved."

Moe considered the ruthlessly pragmatic proposal, knowing it gave the corrupt commissioners a light at the end of the tunnel compared to the nuclear option of prosecution. He gave Woodson a reluctant nod. "You've got a deal - but only if every penny gets paid back plus interest. And any whiff of them not playing ball gets reported up the line immediately."

In the end, Woodson's hardball strategy paid off - at least for keeping the

Transit Commission's gears turning smoothly. Once slapped with the cold truth and unassailable evidence Moe had compiled, the three commissioners played ball. They issued undated resignations, paid back over $17 million in illicit funds to the municipal coffers, and slunk away into disgraced silence.

The whole underworld shakedown and rectification played out in a few surgical weeks, never seeing the light of lurid public scrutiny. While not the pound-of-flesh justice that prosecutor part of Moe has craved, he took solace in the clear-eyed realities.

The unconscionable blight had been purged from the city's Transit Authority with finality and not a single penny had been ultimately left unpaid. As Commissioner Woodson gripped Moe's hand in his meaty paw, he made it clear this sort of indispensable, if discretionary

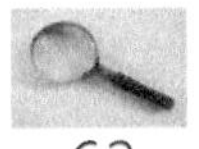

expertise, would continue being tapped for years to come.

"Don't get too cozy in your East LA office once we get some fresh blood reseated over at TAC," Woodson said with a grim chuckle. "I've got a feeling I'll be beckoning you into more than a few back-alley diners before your PI days are done, Juarez."

Moe already knew it was true. For every upstanding official and civic institution, there were seemingly two more operators itching to carve off a slice of the pie for themselves to devour - regardless of what innocent civilians got caught in the crosshairs.

As long as men stayed imperfect, giving into greed and vices, the darkness would keep spreading - be it on skid row back alleys or the marbled heights of the city's structural capillaries. Moe's services as a veritable surgeon would

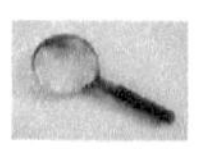

forever be in dire need, lancing each new corruption wherever it inevitably took putrid root.

It wasn't a glamorous or valorous calling by any stretch. But in that moment with Woodson, gripping his hand with a seasoned sense of dogged purpose, Moe knew he wouldn't have had it any other way. He was one of the city's few honest men brave enough to wield the scalpel - and someone had to keep wielding it, no matter how hazardous or bleak the operating theater turned.

The staggering Transit Authority graft case proved to Moe "Snake-Eyes" Juarez that no civic institution was truly impervious to the insidious spread of corruption. But even he couldn't have anticipated just how deep and high up the human appetite for exploiting power could burrow.

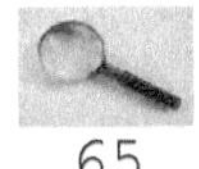

The Grocery Store Heist

In Moe's office the pungent odors of Cuban coffee and cheap rum wafted up the rickety stairs. Moe kept the windows open to try to catch whatever whispers of a breeze might pass through.

The door slammed open and Moe's latest client barged in, a sweaty mess in an ill-fitting suit. This was Eduardo Ramirez, owner of a small grocery store over on Whittier Boulevard. Two nights ago, somebody had busted through his front window and cleaned out the cash register.

"Find who did this, Snake-Eyes!" Ramirez demanded, using Moe's street nickname from his gambling days. "I need that money to pay for my child's medicine!"

Moe nodded wearily. "Don't worry, Mr. Ramirez. I'll lean on a few of my snitches, see what shakes loose."

His next case came walking in the very next day. This was a beautiful young lady named Dolores, tears staining her heavily made-up face. It was a case of a missing husband - he'd gone off pursuing a get-rich-quick scheme and never returned.

Dolores wrung her hands nervously. "Please, Mr. Juarez, you have to find him! I need him to come home. I'm...I'm pregnant."

Moe felt a pang in his chest. He'd always had a soft spot for dames in trouble. "Don't you fret, Miss Dolores. Ol' Snake-Eyes will have your man back before that bun is fully baked."

Over the days that followed, Moe worked both cases tirelessly. He greased palms from East LA to Watts, leaned on snitches and hustlers, and finally caught the break he'd been looking for...

Over the days that followed, Moe worked both cases tirelessly. He greased palms

from East LA to Watts, leaned on snitches and hustlers, and finally caught the break he'd been looking for.

Ramirez's grocery burglary was solved first. Through some very persuasive "interviews," Moe discovered it was the work of a punk kid named Jacinto and his gang of mallet-headed gang members. They'd been going around smashing and grabbing from mom-and-pop stores to fund their weed and booze habits. Moe paid them a late-night visit, cracking a couple skulls until they coughed up Ramirez's cash box. The grocer was overjoyed when Moe returned the money.

Dolores' missing husband case took longer. Finally, a greased palm got Moe a lead - the hubby, Hector, had gotten mixed up with a bad crowd running cross-border scams. They'd lured him in with promises of quick riches, then gotten him

involved in smuggling hot goods down from
LA to Tijuana.

When Hector got cold feet and tried to
back out, the cartel goons held him for
ransom down in a rat-trap safe house near
the border. Moe saddled up and rode down
to TJ, skirting the federales by making
friends with a few local vice operators.
With their help, he located the safe
house, kicked in the door, and got the
drop on the stunned guards.

"Lookin' for a guy named Hector," Moe
growled, fanning the hammer on his .38.
"Way I hear it, he's a little late to the
padre's barbecue, if you know what I
mean."

The guards squealed like stuck pigs and
soon Moe had Hector freed, a little
roughed up but alive. He brought the
missing husband home to a grateful,
tearfully relieved Dolores. She damn near
broke Moe's ribs with her hug.

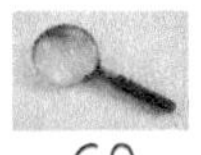

As Hector and his wife celebrated their reunion, Moe ducked out and headed back to his office, already pondering the next case. East LA was a baking kettle of troubles, and Snake-Eyes Juarez was keeping the lid on tight.

Maria's Missing Papers

After solving the cases of Ramirez's burgled grocery and Dolores' missing husband, life briefly returned to normal for Moe "Snake-Eyes" Juarez in his East LA office. But it wouldn't last long in this city - trouble always came knocking. Sure enough, a new client pushed through Moe's door a few days later. This was Maria Vega, the wife of a wealthy businessman. She wore an expensive fur coat despite the stifling summer heat. "Mr. Juarez, I need you to find something for me," Maria said breathily,

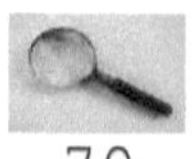

momentarily fanning herself. "An item of great value that's gone missing."

Moe leaned back in his creaky chair. "I'm listenin', Mrs. Vega. What's got those pearl necklaces of yours in a twist?"

Maria glanced around furtively before leaning in close. "It's a set of documents - ledgers and paperwork detailing all my husband's business dealings over the years. Export records, contacts, bank transactions, everything."

"Sounds dicey," Moe noted. "I take it your husband doesn't know you got these files?"

"That's right," Maria admitted. "Ricardo has made many unwise arrangements over the years. If those records were to fall into the wrong hands, it could ruin him."

Moe chewed his cheek. "Lemme guess - you were gonna use 'em as a bargaining chip in the divorce?"

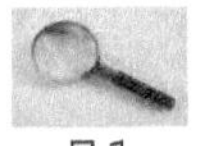

A coy smile played across the woman's ruby lips. "Let's just say I need that leverage, Mr. Juarez. Can you retrieve those papers for me?"

"It'll cost you, doll," Moe warned. "This could get mighty uncomfortable if Rico's mugs get whiff of what I'm doin'."

Maria reached into her coat and pulled out a thick envelope stuffed with crisp bills. "Money is no object, Mr. Juarez. Just get me those files."

Over the next few days, Moe did some digging to trace the missing ledgers. It seemed Maria had stupidly stored them in a rented safe deposit box at a bank downtown - but somebody had gotten there first. Following the trail, Moe realized the perpetrators were members of Rico Vega's inner circle who had gotten wise to Maria's schemes.

The chase led Moe all over the sleazier sections of East LA's underbelly as he

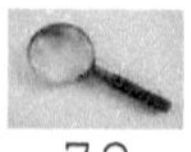

tried to stay one step ahead of Vega's brutal enforcers. He tracked the files from the bank vault to a backroom at a Chinatown gambling parlor, then to a hole-up flat that got raided by Vega's men. Finally, Moe found himself standing in a darkened warehouse at the port, revolvers trained on him from the shadows.

"Should've minded your own business, Juarez!" one of the goons growled.

The darkened warehouse was tensely silent for a moment after the thug's growled warning. Then all hell broke loose in a deafening barrage of gunfire.

Moe dropped to the ground, his fedora knocked askew as bullets whined and ricocheted all around him. He snapped off a couple quick shots from his .38. One of Vega's gorillas went down clutching his leg.

Using an upturned wooden crate as cover, Moe made his way towards the far end of the warehouse, trading shots with the hired muscle. He could make out at least three of them, possibly more lying in wait to ambush him. The thick air was choked with acrid cordite smoke.

Suddenly, one of the goons came bucking out of the shadows, swinging a length of lead pipe at Moe's head. The PI ducked and the pipe clanged off the crate, splinters flying. Moe put two burning slugs into the man's chest and he crumpled with a muffled groan.

"You're just making this harder on yourself, snake-eyes!" one of the other muscle-boys shouted from his concealed position.

Moe risked a peek over the crate's edge and that's when he saw it - the battered briefcase lying a few yards away, half-obscured by shadows. Those must be Vega's

incriminating files! If he could just make a play to scoop them up...

Drawing a deep breath, Moe burst from his cover and made a headlong scramble for the briefcase, stitching the warehouse with wild shots from the automatic. Up ahead, one of Vega's last goons broke from cover, charging at Moe with a Tommy gun barking lines of blazing tracers.

Time seemed to slow in that endless moment. Moe could see every spark and flare from the gangster's gun muzzle. He threw himself into a desperate slide, feeling the burning smash of bullets kicking into the concrete all around him. His pistol was out of ammo, but he could see the goon's eyes widen as Moe slammed into him, carrying them both to the grimy floor.

They wrestled and grappled, fists and elbows and knees flying in a frenzy of violence. Moe got slashed by a knife

before he could finally pound the man's skull into the concrete until he stopped moving. Battered and bloodied, the PI slumped back, chest heaving.

He'd retrieved Vega's files...but at what cost? Moe didn't know if he'd be able to walk out of this godforsaken warehouse. He only hoped Maria's damning papers would be worth the price he paid.

The Horn Man is Missing

The midday sun beat down on Whittier Boulevard, turning the East L.A. asphalt into a shimmering mirage. Inside his cramped office, Moe "Snake Eyes" Juarez mopped his brow with a handkerchief. The whirring of a ceiling fan offered little relief. Business, like the weather, was stagnant.

A rap on the scratched wooden door startled him. Moe straightened his tie,

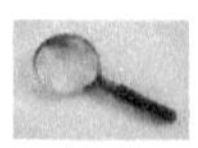

a garish green number that clashed
spectacularly with his seersucker suit.
A woman, all curves and worry lines,
stood at the threshold. Her name was
Dolores Sanchez, and her husband,
Roberto, a prominent trumpet player with
a penchant for late-night jam sessions,
hadn't come home in two days.
"He wouldn't just leave, Mr. Juarez,"
Dolores pleaded, her voice thick with
tears. "He had a big gig next week. New
suit, the whole thing."
Moe listened patiently, his eyes, as
sharp as the nickname they earned him,
taking in the details - the tremor in
Dolores' hands, the desperation clinging
to her like a cheap perfume. He poured
her a glass of amber liquid from a dusty
bottle on his desk. "Cactus juice," he
explained with a wink. "Not for the faint
of heart, but it loosens tongues faster
than a bar fight."

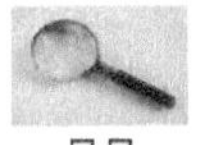

Dolores downed the fiery concoction, coughing slightly. "Roberto wouldn't stray," she insisted, her voice gaining a touch of defiance. "Not for another woman, not with that big gig coming up." A spark flickered in Moe's eyes. "Another woman, huh? Did Roberto have any… admirers?"

Dolores sniffed. "There was this redhead at the Club Intimo. Always hanging around after his sets, batting her eyelashes like a caught butterfly."

The Club Intimo. A notorious jazz club known for its smoky atmosphere and clientele with more secrets than a priest's confession box. This was a lead, a whiff of something more sinister than a marital spat.

That night, Moe, clad in a black fedora pulled low over his brow, slipped into the Club Intimo. The air hung heavy with cigarette smoke and the rhythmic wail of

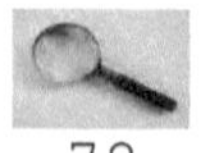

a saxophone. He scanned the dimly lit room, his gaze finally landing on a fiery-haired woman perched on a barstool, a half-empty glass of whiskey clutched in her hand.

"Dolores mentioned a redhead," Moe slid onto the stool next to her, his voice a low murmur.

The woman turned her emerald eyes narrowed. "And who might Dolores be?"

"A concerned wife," Moe replied coolly. "Looking for her missing trumpet-playing husband."

The redhead scoffed. "Roberto Sanchez? He left of his own accord, sweetheart. Couldn't handle the heat."

"Heat?" Moe raised an eyebrow. "You mean something besides the habanero salsa?"

The redhead's smile faltered. "Look, pal, I don't know what Roberto told his wife, but he owed some fellas some money. Gambling debts, you understand."

Gambling debts. A missing musician with a penchant for late nights and a taste for trouble. The pieces were starting to fall into place.

The next morning, Moe found himself in a back alley, the stench of garbage and desperation thick in the air. He was there to meet "Big Sal," a hulking man with a shaved head and a temper to match. Sal, it turned out, was the one Roberto owed money to.

"You think you can strongarm my money back, Juarez?" Sal boomed, a gold tooth glinting in the morning sun.

"Not exactly," Moe said, his voice steady despite the tremor in his stomach. "But Roberto skipped town, leaving his most prized possession behind."

He reached into his worn briefcase and pulled out Roberto's gleaming trumpet, the instrument a stark contrast to the grimy surroundings. Sal's eyes widened.

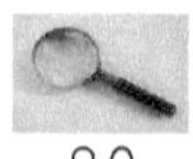

That trumpet was Roberto's lifeblood, worth more than any gambling debt.

A tense negotiation ensued, punctuated by Sal's meaty fists slamming on a nearby crate. In the end, a deal was struck. The trumpet for Roberto's freedom, with a stern warning to never gamble again.

Moe returned to Dolores' house that evening, the trumpet held high like a trophy. Dolores' face lit up with relief. Roberto, sheepish but safe, emerged from a back room, the sounds of his warm trumpet filling the air shortly after.

Word of Moe's success spread like wildfire through the East L.A. grapevine. Soon, his office door was revolving with a cast of characters - a jealous baker whose wife was smitten with the milkman, a nervous boxer afraid of the upcoming fight, a group of neighborhood kids convinced a local magician was harboring a stolen parrot.

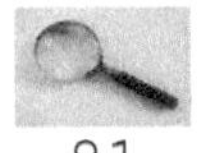

The Missing Silver Candelabra

The next client to walk through Moe's door was a man as stiff as a freshly starched collar and about as colorful. Mr. Huntington Higginbottom III, heir to the Higginbottom Silver fortune, fidgeted with his starched cuffs as he explained his predicament. A priceless silver candelabra, a family heirloom, had vanished from his heavily guarded mansion.

The mansion, perched high on a hill overlooking the city, reeked of privilege and stale air conditioning. Moe, sweating through his suit in the opulent foyer, surveyed the scene. The security system was state-of-the-art, the windows were locked tight, and the staff, a gaggle of nervous maids and a jittery butler, all swore innocence.

Something wasn't adding up. The mansion felt like a gilded cage, the staff

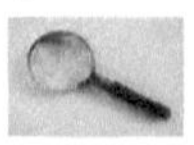

walking on eggshells around Mr. Higginbottom, who seemed more concerned about the candelabra's monetary value than its sentimental worth.

Moe spent a day poking around the mansion, his keen eyes noticing a chipped vase no one seemed to care about and a faint smudge of silver polish on a back staircase. He interviewed the staff one by one, his gruff demeanor softened by a shared pack of Lucky Strikes with the gruff but kind-hearted cook, Mrs. Hernandez.

Finally, a breakthrough. Mrs. Hernandez, her weathered face creased with worry, confessed to seeing a young maid, barely out of her teens, leaving the mansion late one night with a bulky package. The girl, new and skittish, had vanished without a trace.

Following this lead, Moe found himself in a rundown tenement building, a stark

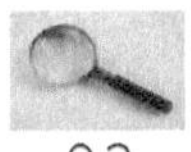

contrast to the Higginbottom mansion. He located the missing maid, huddled in a cramped apartment, surrounded by a family struggling to put food on the table.

The story unfolded. The girl, desperate to help her ailing father, had seen the candelabra as a way out. She hadn't planned on stealing it, but the opportunity had presented itself during a late-night cleaning shift.

Moe, touched by the girl's plight, devised a plan. He confronted Mr. Higginbottom, presenting him with a stark choice - press charges against the girl, ruining her life, or use his wealth to help her family and consider the candelabra a donation.

Mr. Higginbottom, initially outraged, balked at the idea. But Moe, with a steely glint in his eyes, reminded him of the good publicity such a gesture would

generate. In the end, Mr. Higginbottom, with a grimace, agreed to Moe's terms.

The candelabra returned to the Higginbottom mansion, albeit with a slightly different story attached. The girl received the medical care her father desperately needed, and Moe, once again, found himself a champion of the underdog in the glittering, yet often unforgiving, city of East Los Angeles.

News of Moe's success spread further, reaching the ears of a nervous young boxer named "Kid Lightning" Lopez. Kid Lightning, a rising star on the East L.A. boxing scene, was scheduled for a title fight against a notorious bully known as "Iron Mike" Maloney. Fear gnawed at the young boxer, threatening to derail his dreams.

Kid Lightning, a bundle of nervous energy barely contained within his oversized robe, confessed to Moe that he was being

threatened by Iron Mike's goons. They were pressuring him to throw the fight, a tactic as common as a left hook in the underbelly of the boxing world.

Moe, a boxing enthusiast in his younger days, knew the fight game had a dark side. He agreed to help Kid Lightning, not by coaching him in the ring, but by evening the odds outside it.

Days leading up to the fight, Moe became Kid Lightning's shadow. He scared off thugs lurking outside his gym, intercepted threatening messages, and even convinced a friendly bartender to slip a laxative into Iron Mike's pre-fight protein shake (a detail Moe conveniently left out of his official report).

The night of the fight arrived, electric with anticipation. Kid Lightning, fear replaced by a steely determination, entered the ring. Iron Mike, sluggish and

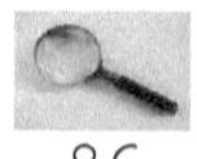

irritable thanks to Moe's "intervention," lumbered after him.

The fight was a spectacle. Kid Lightning, nimble and fueled by a newfound confidence, danced around Iron Mike, landing sharp jabs and lightning-fast hooks. The crowd, initially skeptical, roared with approval as the underdog dominated the ring.

In the end, it was a unanimous decision - Kid Lightning, the people's champion, emerged victorious. Iron Mike, his face a mask of disbelief and a hint of nausea, slunk out of the ring.

Moe, watching from the shadows, felt a surge of pride. He wasn't just a private investigator; he was a weaver of justice, a guardian angel in a rumpled suit navigating the moral gray areas of East L.A. His reputation as a man who got things done, not always by the book but

always with a keen sense of right and wrong, solidified.

The Archaeologist Has Gone Missing

One sweltering afternoon, a woman with an air of faded elegance walked into Moe's office. Her name was Evelyn Thorne, and her problem was as cold as the diamonds adorning her trembling hands. Her son, Alistair, a renowned archaeologist obsessed with Mayan artifacts, had vanished during an expedition deep in the jungles of Guatemala.

The official search party had returned empty-handed, deeming Alistair lost or worse. But Evelyn, a woman of unwavering determination, refused to give up. She believed Alistair was still alive, a prisoner of some unknown force.

The case was unlike anything Moe had faced before. It wasn't about stolen valuables or jealous lovers, but about

the mysteries of a lost civilization and the dangers lurking in the heart of the jungle. Intrigued and touched by Evelyn's unwavering love for her son, Moe decided to take on the case.

His investigation led him to dusty libraries and smoky backrooms filled with rum-soaked adventurers and jaded treasure hunters. He pieced together a story of a hidden Mayan temple rumored to hold unimaginable riches, guarded by deadly traps and a fierce indigenous tribe protecting their ancestral lands. Alistair, consumed by his obsession, had ventured deeper into the jungle than anyone dared, following whispers of the temple's location. Now, he was lost, a captive of this forgotten world.

Assembling a ragtag team of experts – a wizened Mayan translator, a grizzled ex-military guide, and a smuggler with a shady past but a keen knowledge of the

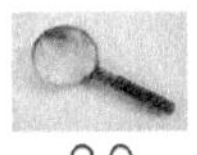

Guatemalan terrain - Moe embarked on a perilous journey into the heart of the jungle.

Days blurred into weeks as they hacked their way through dense undergrowth, braved torrential downpours, and faced the dangers of the wild. The translator deciphered ancient glyphs carved into crumbling ruins, leading them closer to the hidden temple.

Finally, they reached a clearing shrouded in mist. A magnificent Mayan temple, its once vibrant colors faded by time, rose before them. But guarding the entrance was a fierce tribe, their faces painted with war paint, their eyes filled with suspicion.

Through the translator, Moe explained their mission - not to plunder the temple's treasures, but to rescue a lost man. A tense standoff ensued, punctuated

by guttural chants and the brandishing of primitive weapons.

Just as it seemed all was lost, Evelyn, who had insisted on accompanying them despite the dangers, stepped forward. She held up a worn photograph, a picture of a young Alistair smiling next to a Mayan child.

The photograph, a reminder of a past cultural exchange Alistair had participated in, sparked a flicker of recognition in the tribe leader's eyes. A low murmur rippled through the crowd, followed by a single nod.

They were granted passage. Inside the temple, they found Alistair, not as a prisoner, but as a guest. He had befriended the tribe, sharing his knowledge of Mayan culture and earning their respect.

The reunion between Evelyn and Alistair was tearful and joyous. Together, they

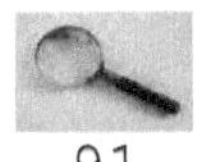

emerged from the temple, not with stolen artifacts, but with a newfound understanding and respect for the Mayan people and their sacred temple.

News of Moe's daring rescue and his role in fostering cultural understanding spread far and wide. He became a legend, not just for solving cases, but for venturing beyond the expected, proving that sometimes the greatest treasures weren't gold or jewels, but the bonds of friendship forged in the most unexpected places.

Missing Priceless Heirloom Necklace

Back in his office, the whirring of the fan a comforting constant, Moe looked out at the bustling streets of East L.A. The city, a kaleidoscope of dreams and struggles, continued its continuous march forward. And Moe "Snake Eyes" Juarez, the rumpled private investigator

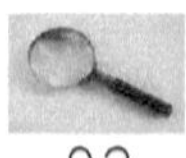

with a heart of gold, would be there, ready to face whatever mystery or injustice walked through his door.

A nervous-looking young woman, barely out of her teens, burst through the door. Her name was Sylvia Delgado, and her predicament involved a missing necklace - not just any necklace, but a priceless heirloom passed down through generations in her family. The necklace, a delicate silver chain adorned with a luminescent opal, had vanished from her apartment the night before.

"It was like it vanished into thin air, Mr. Juarez," Sylvia stammered, her voice trembling. "The door was locked, the windows were shut, and there were no signs of a break-in."

Moe listened patiently, his keen eyes taking in the details - the worry etched across Sylvia's face, the worn leather purse clutched tightly in her hands. He

93

offered her a glass of cool lemonade, a welcome respite from the oppressive heat.
"Did anyone have access to your apartment? A friend, a boyfriend?"
Sylvia blushed slightly. "There was Miguel, the delivery guy from the bakery downstairs. He's kind of cute, and..." she trailed off, embarrassment coloring her cheeks.
A delivery guy, huh? Intriguing. While petty theft wasn't uncommon, a missing heirloom with sentimental value suggested something more. Moe decided to pay a visit to the bakery downstairs.
The bakery, a haven of sweet smells and bustling activity, was owned by a gruff but kind-hearted man named Antonio. Miguel, the delivery guy, turned out to be a skinny teenager with an endearingly awkward smile.
"Miguel wouldn't steal anything, Mr. Juarez," Antonio boomed, his voice thick

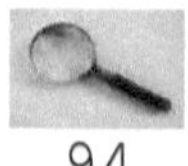

with a heavy Italian accent. "He's a good kid, comes from a good family."

However, Miguel's nervousness under Moe's questioning was hard to miss. He kept shifting his weight, his eyes darting around the room. Finally, with a deep breath, he confessed.

He hadn't stolen the necklace. He'd seen it lying on Sylvia's table one day and, captivated by its beauty, had taken it to a local pawn shop. He intended to buy it back, but the pawnbroker had offered him a sum he desperately needed to help his ailing grandmother.

Sylvia, upon hearing Miguel's tearful confession, surprised everyone. She didn't press charges. Instead, she saw the desperation in his eyes, a reflection of the struggles many faced in the harsh realities of East L.A.

Moe, touched by Sylvia's compassion, hatched a plan. He borrowed some money

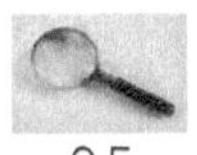

from Antonio, enough to redeem the necklace and help Miguel's grandmother. In return, Sylvia agreed to tutor Miguel, offering him a chance to improve his English and future prospects.

The case concluded with an unlikely friendship blossoming between Sylvia and Miguel, the stolen necklace a symbol of not just loss, but of unexpected kindness and a helping hand. Moe, watching them leave his office, a flicker of warmth lit his eyes. He wasn't just a solver of mysteries; he was a weaver of unexpected connections, a testament to the resilience of the human spirit even in the face of adversity.

The Lucky Theft

The next client to walk through his door was a portly man with a neatly trimmed mustache and a worried frown. His name was Mr. Bartholomew Finch, a film

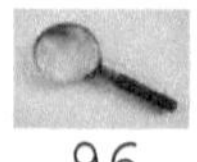

producer from Hollywood. He had a problem - a script, the crown jewel of his upcoming production, had vanished from his office safe.

The script, penned by a reclusive writer known only as "The Shadow," was rumored to be a surefire hit. Its disappearance threatened to derail the entire production and Mr. Finch's career.

The case plunged Moe into the glamorous yet treacherous world of Hollywood. He navigated through a labyrinth of jealous actors, disgruntled crew members, and a flamboyant director with a penchant for flamboyant accusations. Everyone seemed to have a motive, and the whispers of sabotage hung thick in the air.

Days turned into weeks as Moe sifted through alibis, interviewed suspects, and even spent a night tailing a suspicious-looking screenwriter with a grudge against The Shadow. The trail grew

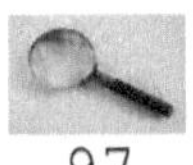

cold, frustration mounting with each dead end.

Finally, a breakthrough. A sharp-eyed security guard remembered seeing a young intern, an aspiring writer himself, lingering near Mr. Finch's office on the night of the theft. The intern, a nervous young man named Harold, confessed under Moe's questioning.

Harold hadn't stolen the script to sell it. He, a frustrated and unrecognized writer, had simply dreamt of reading a masterpiece, a chance to glean the secrets of The Shadow's brilliance. He'd planned to return the script after a quick perusal, a naive act fueled by a yearning for inspiration.

Mr. Finch, initially furious, surprised everyone with his next move. He saw potential in Harold, a spark of raw talent overshadowed by self-doubt. He offered Harold a chance - a mentorship

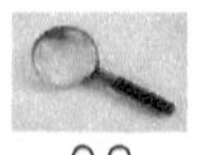

from a seasoned script doctor and a rewrite opportunity for a low-budget film.

Harold, overwhelmed with gratitude, returned the script, his dreams now fueled by a legitimate path forward. Mr. Finch, with a newfound respect for raw talent, embarked on a production with a renewed sense of purpose. Moe, witnessing an unlikely mentorship blossom, felt a familiar sense of satisfaction. He wasn't just solving cases; he was creating opportunities, nudging people towards a brighter future.

Philomena got a Cracker?

The next case that landed on his desk was a doozy - a missing parrot, not just any parrot, but a prized possession of a notorious gangster named "Diamond" Dino Salucci. The parrot, a squawking green monstrosity named Philomena, was rumored

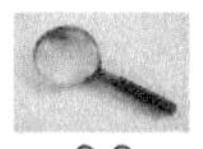

to be worth a small fortune and possessed
an uncanny ability to mimic incriminating
conversations.

The gangster's world was a far cry from
the Hollywood glitz or the desperate
struggles Moe usually navigated. It was
a world of violence, veiled threats, and
hidden loyalties. Moe, entering a dimly
lit night club that served as Salucci's
unofficial headquarters, felt a knot of
unease tighten in his stomach.

Salucci, a burly man with a diamond pinky
ring the size of a walnut, greeted Moe
with a chilling smile. His words were
laced with menace as he explained the
importance of Philomena. Without the
parrot, the feds wouldn't have a leg to
stand on in their upcoming case against
him.

The investigation led Moe into a seedy
underworld of backroom gambling dens and
shady characters who spoke in hushed

tones and kept their eyes nervously shifting. He learned about a rival gang, "The Purple Cobras," known for their ruthlessness and their fondness for exotic birds.

The trail led him to a ramshackle building on the outskirts of town, a known hangout for the Cobras. Inside, amidst a haze of cigarette smoke and cheap whiskey, Moe found Philomena perched on a greasy pole, squawking obscenities and mimicking the voice of a particularly irate police captain.

The leader of the Cobras, a wiry man with a handlebar mustache and a pet snake coiled around his arm, emerged from the shadows. It turned out the parrot wasn't stolen; it had flown the coop, literally, and landed in their territory.

Negotiations were tense, punctuated by the occasional hiss from the leader's pet snake. In the end, a deal was struck —

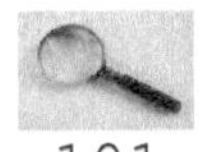

the parrot would be returned in exchange
for Moe overlooking a minor
"misunderstanding" involving a shipment
of "borrowed" sugar (a euphemism for
illegal liquor).

Back at Salucci's night club, the
gangster received his prized parrot with
a grudging nod of thanks. Moe, relieved
to be out of the gangster's world,
slipped away before any further
"misunderstandings" could arise.

As the city lights twinkled outside his
window that night, Moe reflected on the
day's events. He wasn't just a private
investigator; he was a bridge between
disparate worlds, a facilitator of
unexpected deals, and a guardian of sorts
in the often-unruly tapestry of East L.A.
life. He may not have solved world-ending
crimes, but he brought resolution to the
small injustices and tangled situations
that made up the everyday struggles of

the city's inhabitants. And in that, Moe
"Snake Eyes" Juarez found a purpose as
unwavering as the sun that beat down on
the bustling streets of his beloved East
L.A.

Where oh Where has My Whiskers Gone?
Inside his cluttered office, Moe "Snake
Eyes" Juarez dabbed his brow with his
handkerchief that had seen better days.
The whirring fan seemed to mock him,
offering little comfort in the stifling
heat. Business, however, was booming. A
middle-aged woman with worry etched into
her features burst through the door. Her
name was Amelia Cartwright, and her
problem involved a missing person - her
beloved cat, Whiskers.
Whiskers wasn't just any cat; he was a
ginger tabby with a penchant for napping
in sunbeams and an uncanny ability to
predict rain by staring intently out the

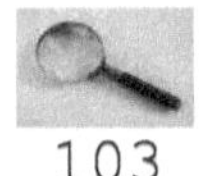

103

window. Amelia, a lonely spinster who lived alone, considered Whiskers her closest companion.

"He's never gone missing before, Mr. Juarez," Amelia said, her voice thick with emotion. "I've checked everywhere. I've put up posters, called the shelters, even left out a bowl of tuna by the door." Moe listened patiently, his keen eyes taking in the details - the tremor in Amelia's hands, the worn photograph of a ginger tabby clutched tightly in her grasp. He offered her a glass of cool iced tea, a welcome respite from the oppressive heat.

"Did you have any recent visitors, Mrs. Cartwright? Anyone unfamiliar?"

Amelia thought for a moment. "There was a young boy from down the street. Billy, his name is. He loves cats and always tries to play with Whiskers when he sees him outside."

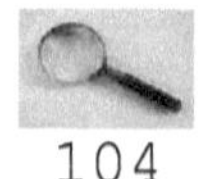

A young boy, huh? Intriguing. While the idea of a child stealing a cat wasn't uncommon, the desperation in Amelia's eyes suggested something more. Moe decided to pay a visit to young Billy.

He found Billy in a nearby park, engrossed in a game of catch with a scruffy mutt. The boy, all freckled skin and boundless energy, greeted Moe with a gap-toothed grin.

"Whiskers? No sir, haven't seen him," Billy chirped, his voice full of genuine confusion.

However, Moe noticed a slight tremor in Billy's voice, a flicker of something akin to fear in his eyes. He knelt down to Billy's level, his voice gentle but firm.

"Billy, sometimes when we love something a lot, we might do things we know are wrong. Did you maybe take Whiskers somewhere to keep him safe?"

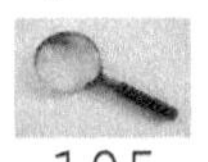

Billy's eyes welled up with tears. He confessed that he'd seen a stray dog chasing Whiskers the other day and, fearing for the cat's safety, had lured him into his house with a can of tuna. He kept Whiskers hidden in his basement, scared to return him and face Amelia's disappointment.

Moe, touched by Billy's concern for Whiskers, hatched a plan. He took Billy back to Amelia's house, where the tearful reunion between the cat and his owner melted even Moe's gruff exterior. Billy, relieved and forgiven, promised to be more honest in the future.

The case concluded with an unlikely friendship blossoming between Amelia and Billy, their shared love for Whiskers bridging the gap between their generations. Moe, watching them walk away together, a content smile playing on his lips, knew his job wasn't just about

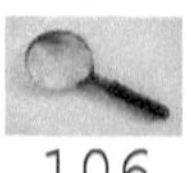

solving mysteries. It was about weaving connections, fostering understanding, and reminding people of the simple joys found in unexpected places.

The Case of the Forged Van Gogh

The next knock on his door brought a whiff of expensive cologne and a sense of urgency. A well-dressed man with slicked-back hair and a manicured mustache introduced himself as Mr. Davenport, a high-profile art collector. His problem - a priceless Van Gogh painting, the centerpiece of his collection, had been replaced with a near-perfect forgery.

The case plunged Moe into the high-stakes world of art auctions, shady dealers, and meticulous forgers. He delved into the history of the painting, interviewed art experts, and even spent a night tailing a shifty-looking art critic with a gambling habit. The pressure was on - Mr.

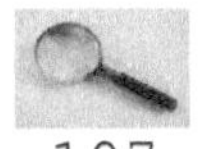

Davenport was willing to pay a hefty sum to recover his stolen masterpiece.

Days turned into weeks as Moe sifted through clues, alibis, and a labyrinth of art jargon that left him feeling like a fish out of water. The trail grew cold, frustration mounting with each dead end. Just as he was about to give up, a chance encounter at a local bar proved fortuitous.

He overheard two men, reeking of cheap whiskey and desperation, discussing a "big score" involving a "phony Gogh." Following them discreetly, Moe found himself at a rundown warehouse on the docks. Inside, under a dim light, a man with calloused hands meticulously touched up a copy of a Van Gogh sunflower painting.

The confrontation was tense. Moe, his hand hovering near his holster, identified himself and ordered the men to

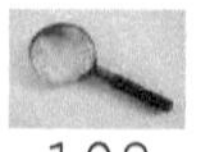

108

drop their brushes. The forger, a wiry man with a haunted look in his eyes, surrendered readily. His accomplice, a burly ex-boxer with a cauliflower ear, hesitated, his hand twitching near his pocket.

A tense silence stretched between them, broken only by the dripping of condensation from a leaky pipe overhead. Moe, sensing the boxer's fear, lowered his voice, a hint of empathy replacing the usual gruffness.

"It doesn't have to end like this," he said. "This guy," he gestured towards the forger, "he has talent. Real talent. Stealing won't help him."

The forger spoke for the first time, his voice raspy. "Talent doesn't pay the bills, mister. Not like a quick buck for a good fake."

Moe saw an opening. "Look," he said, "I understand. But there are people who

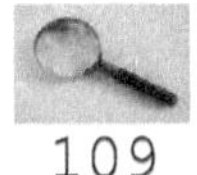

appreciate real talent. People who would pay good money for your work, honestly." He explained Mr. Davenport's collection, his genuine love for art. He spoke of the forger's potential, of galleries and exhibitions, a future built on his own skills. The boxer, surprised by Moe's unexpected words, remained silent, his gaze flitting between Moe and his partner.

Finally, the forger sighed, a flicker of hope lighting up his eyes. He agreed to cooperate, to create a new, authentic piece for Mr. Davenport in exchange for a clean slate and a chance to showcase his talent.

News of the recovered painting, albeit not the original, spread like wildfire. Mr. Davenport, impressed by the forger's genuine talent and touched by Moe's unorthodox approach, agreed to sponsor an exhibition showcasing the forger's work.

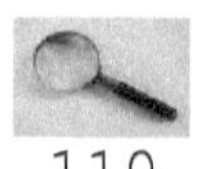

The stolen painting, now safely back in the hands of the police, became a cautionary tale, a footnote overshadowed by the rise of a newfound artistic star. The forger, no longer a criminal but an artist on the rise, stood at the opening of his exhibition, a sense of gratitude etched on his face. Mr. Davenport, beaming with pride at his unorthodox investment, shook Moe's hand firmly.

As the city lights twinkled outside his window that night, Moe reflected on the day's events. He wasn't just a private investigator; he was a catalyst for change, a champion for the underdog, and a weaver of unexpected second chances. He may not have solved world-ending crimes, but he had helped rewrite the narratives of those around him, proving that even in the heart of a bustling city, redemption and a glimmer of hope could bloom in the most unexpected places.

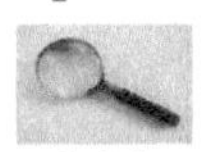

Rosalind's Scientist is Missing

Inside his cluttered office, Moe "Snake Eyes" Juarez dabbed his brow with his handkerchief, the once vibrant pattern now faded with age. The whirring fan seemed to mock him, offering little comfort in the stifling heat.

A nervous tremor ran through the woman who burst through the door next. Her name was Rosalind Hughes, and her predicament involved a missing husband, a renowned scientist named Dr. Arthur Hughes, who had vanished without a trace.

"It's not like Arthur to disappear," Rosalind explained, her voice trembling. "He's meticulous, always leaves detailed notes, especially when working on a big project."

Dr. Hughes, on the cusp of a breakthrough cancer treatment, had been working tirelessly in his home lab. The night before, Rosalind had found his lab empty,

his notes scattered across the floor, and a single, cryptic message scrawled on the whiteboard: "They know."

The case plunged Moe into the world of high-stakes scientific research, ruthless competitors, and government conspiracies. He interviewed colleagues, some tight-lipped and fearful, others suspiciously eager to see Dr. Hughes' project fail. He delved into the complex world of cellular biology, his head spinning from terms like "oncogenes" and "apoptosis."

Days turned into weeks as Moe sifted through clues, alibis, and a labyrinth of scientific jargon that left him feeling like a fish out of water. The trail grew cold, frustration mounting with each dead end. Just as he was about to hit another wall, a seemingly random conversation at a local diner sparked a connection.

An elderly waitress, known for her sharp wit and even sharper memory, mentioned a heated argument she overheard a few nights back. It involved two men, one with a distinguished air, the other burly and vaguely menacing, talking about silencing someone and "shutting down that rogue project."

The distinguished man fit the description of Dr. Thompson, a rival scientist known for his cutthroat tactics and skepticism towards Dr. Hughes' groundbreaking research. Following a hunch, Moe decided to pay Dr. Thompson a visit.

Dr. Thompson, a man with an air of icy superiority, scoffed at the suggestion of foul play. He readily admitted to the argument, claiming it was a heated debate about scientific merit, nothing more. But Moe, his gut churning with suspicion, noticed a flicker of nervousness in Dr. Thompson's eyes, a telltale sign.

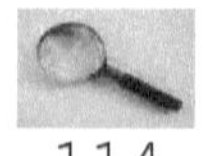

Later that night, staking out Dr. Thompson's mansion, Moe witnessed a clandestine meeting. Thompson was talking to two burly men, the same ones the waitress had described. They were loading what looked like scientific equipment into a nondescript van.

The pieces clicked into place. Dr. Thompson, fearing Dr. Hughes' success would overshadow his own work, had hired thugs to kidnap the scientist and steal his research. Armed with this knowledge, Moe formulated a daring plan.

The next morning, he contacted Rosalind, explaining his suspicions and the need for a diversion. Rosalind, a woman of remarkable courage, agreed to play a part. She staged a dramatic "breakdown" at Dr. Thompson's doorstep, accusing him of stealing her husband's research.

The commotion caused by Rosalind's outburst created the perfect opportunity

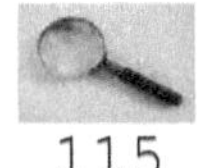

for Moe to sneak into Dr. Thompson's mansion. He navigated through sterile labs filled with high-tech equipment, finally locating a hidden basement where Dr. Hughes was being held captive.

A tense standoff ensued. Moe, outnumbered but undeterred, bluffed his way through the situation, using his knowledge of police procedure (mostly gleaned from bad detective novels) to intimidate the thugs. In the ensuing confusion, Dr. Hughes managed to break free and overpower one of his captors.

The police, alerted by Rosalind's act, arrived on the scene just in time. Dr. Thompson was arrested, his dreams of scientific glory crumbling around him. Dr. Hughes, shaken but unharmed, was reunited with his wife in a tearful embrace.

News of Moe's daring rescue and his role in exposing a scientific conspiracy

spread far and wide. He became a beacon of hope for the underdog, a symbol that even in the cutthroat world of scientific research, integrity and courage could prevail.

As Dr. and Mrs. Hughes visited Moe's office to express their gratitude, a sense of quiet satisfaction settled over him. He wasn't just a private investigator; he was a defender of truth, a champion for the voiceless, and a weaver of justice in the bustling tapestry of East L.A. life. The sun dipped below the horizon, casting long shadows across his cluttered desk, but the fire in Moe "Snake Eyes" Juarez's eyes burned bright, a testament to his unwavering dedication to the city and the peculiar cases that landed on his doorstep.

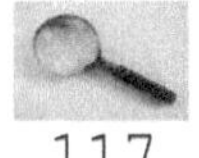

Isabel's Missing Grandmother

The next knock was a tentative one, followed by a hesitant shuffle of feet. A young woman, barely out of her teens, peeked through the doorway. Her name was Isabel Garcia, and worry etched itself into the lines around her eyes despite her youthful face.

"Mr. Juarez," she stammered, clutching a worn photograph, "it's about my Grand Mother. She disappeared."

Moe ushered her in, offering a reassuring smile and a glass of cool water. Isabel explained that her grandmother, a renowned curandera (healer) known throughout the Latino community, had vanished from her home a few days prior. There were no signs of struggle, no forced entry. It was as if she'd simply vanished into thin air.

This case ventured beyond the usual realm of missing persons or stolen valuables.

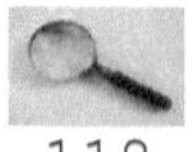

It delved into the mystical beliefs and ancient traditions that ran deep within the heart of East L.A.'s Latino community. Moe, ever the pragmatist, found himself navigating a world of herbal remedies, whispered prayers, and a potent belief in the unseen.

He interviewed Isabel's family, learning of her abuela's reputation for helping those in need, from curing minor ailments to performing intricate spiritual cleansings. He spoke with other curanderos, some wary of outsiders, others offering cryptic advice about malevolent spirits and imbalances in the spiritual realm.

Days turned into weeks, the trail growing colder with each passing sunset. Frustration gnawed at Moe, his usual bravado fading in the face of this perplexing case. Then, one evening, a

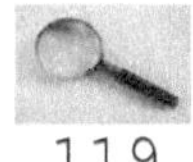

chance encounter at a local botanica (herbal shop) offered a glimmer of hope. An old woman with eyes that held the wisdom of ages spoke of a rare herb, la flor de regreso (the flower of return). Legend said it could guide lost souls back to the physical world, but it only bloomed under a full moon at a hidden location known only to a select few.

Intrigued, Moe followed the woman's cryptic instructions, venturing up into the San Gabriel Canyon to a place called "Shady Oaks" under the cloak of a luminous full moon. The trek was arduous, his path illuminated only by a flickering flashlight. Just as doubt began to creep in, he stumbled upon a clearing bathed in an ethereal glow.

There, nestled amidst ancient ferns, bloomed a single, magnificent flower - la flor de regreso. Carefully, Moe plucked it, a sense of cautious optimism blooming

in his chest. He returned to Isabel, explaining the legend and the flower's potential power.

Isabel, her eyes filled with a newfound determination, took the flower and, along with a group of her abuela's closest friends, performed a traditional ceremony under the light of the next full moon. They chanted ancient prayers, the air thick with the scent of burning sage and exotic incense. As the last notes of the prayer faded, a gasp rippled through the group.

In the distance, a frail figure emerged from the shadows. It was Isabel's grandmother weak but unharmed. She explained a vision, a pull towards a place of healing energy, and a struggle to find her way back.

The reunion between Isabel and her abuela was a tearful one, filled with relief and gratitude. The news of the healer's

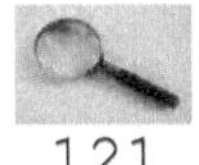

return, aided by a legendary flower and the unwavering love of her family, spread like wildfire. Moe, despite his initial skepticism, found himself touched by the power of faith and the enduring strength of tradition.

Missing Jewels

It was another very hot day on Whittier Boulevard, the sun shimmering off the chrome of a sleek black motorcycle parked haphazardly across the street from Moe's office. Inside, the ever-present whir of the fan offered little respite from the heat, but a faint hum of anticipation crackled in the air.

A woman with a shock of crimson hair and a leather jacket that seemed more defiance than fashion pushed open the door. Her name was Carmen Reyes, and trouble seemed to follow her like a stray cat. She slammed a worn file on Moe's

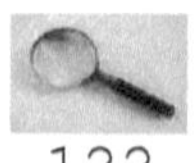

desk, the clatter echoing in the cluttered room.

"Missing jewels," she growled, her voice a smoky rasp. "Not just any jewels, mind you. Family heirlooms with a history as long as this city itself."

Moe eyed the file cautiously. Carmen Reyes, a notorious treasure hunter with a reputation for skirting the legal line, wasn't his usual clientele. But the glint in her steely blue eyes and the desperation etched on her face piqued his curiosity.

He learned the jewels belonged to her estranged grandfather, a man who'd spent his life chasing whispers of buried pirate treasure along the California coast. He'd recently stumbled upon a cryptic map and a legend of a hidden cove guarded by a vengeful spirit before vanishing without a trace.

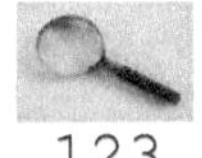

This case plunged Moe into the world of swashbuckling pirates, dusty historical archives, and the murky underbelly of the treasure-hunting community. He navigated treacherous coastlines with Carmen, deciphering faded maps and fending off rival treasure hunters with a penchant for violence. He delved into the city's forgotten past, unearthing stories of pirates, buried gold, and the vengeful spirit of a scorned captain.

Days bled into weeks, the California sun a relentless witness to their pursuit. Dead ends piled up, frustration simmering between Moe and Carmen, their initial distrust slowly giving way to a grudging respect. Just as they were about to call it quits, a chance encounter at a local bar offered a breakthrough.

An old salty dog with a weathered face and a memory sharper than his knife spoke of a hidden cove, accessible only by a

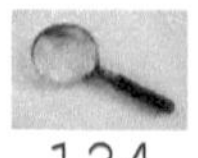

narrow passage during a specific tidal shift. He also mentioned a local legend - the ghost of Captain Pegleg Pete, a ruthless pirate who guarded his buried treasure with a jealous fury.

The pieces clicked into place. Armed with this new information, Moe and Carmen charted a course, the tension thick in the air as they raced against the tide and the whispers of a vengeful spirit. Finally, they reached the hidden cove, a secluded inlet shrouded in an eerie mist. Following the map's cryptic clues, they navigated a treacherous cave system, the air thick with the smell of damp earth and forgotten time. Just as they reached the final chamber, a spectral figure materialized - Captain Pegleg Pete, his ghostly form flickering in the dim light. But this wasn't the vengeful spirit they expected. Captain Pegleg Pete, trapped in an ethereal limbo due to his ill-gotten

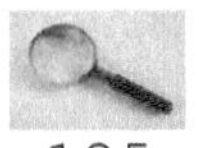

gains, pleaded for his soul to be set free. The only way, he revealed, was to return his stolen love - a simple locket that lay buried with the treasure.

Carmen, touched by the captain's tale and perhaps by a flicker of unexpected compassion, retrieved the locket. As she placed it in the captain's spectral hand, a wave of relief washed over his ghostly form. With a grateful nod, Captain Pegleg Pete faded away, leaving behind a chest overflowing with gold and jewels.

Moe and Carmen returned to the city, their bond forged in the fires of shared danger and unexpected redemption. Carmen, with a newfound respect for her family's legacy, sold a portion of the treasure to fund a local historical society. The rest, she kept, a reminder of her gruff yet surprisingly insightful partner.

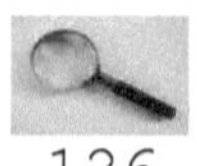

As Carmen walked out of Moe's office, a ghost of a smile playing on her lips, Moe looked out the window at the bustling street. He wasn't just a private investigator; he was a facilitator of lost stories, a bridge between past and present, and a quiet guardian in the ever-shifting tapestry of East L.A. life. The sun dipped below the horizon, casting long shadows across his cluttered desk, but the fire in Moe "Snake Eyes" Juarez's eyes burned bright, a testament to his unwavering dedication to the city's hidden mysteries and the extraordinary people who called it home.

The Case of the Suspicious Masterpiece
Inside Moe's office, the fan whirred a monotonous counterpoint to the rhythmic tapping of a cane. A man with silver hair slicked back and a neatly trimmed goatee stood before Moe's desk, his posture

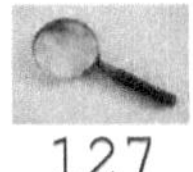

rigid. He introduced himself as Alistair Davenport, a renowned art critic whose reputation preceded him.

"Mr. Juarez," Davenport began, his voice clipped and precise, "I have a most unusual case. It concerns not a missing person or a stolen object, but a forgery so convincing, it has fooled the entire art world."

Intrigued, Moe leaned back in his creaking chair. Art forgeries weren't exactly his forte, but the seriousness etched on Davenport's face piqued his curiosity.

Davenport explained the predicament. A recently discovered painting, attributed to the elusive street artist Banksy, had taken the art world by storm. He, along with other renowned critics, had hailed it as a masterpiece, a testament to Banksy's genius. However, a nagging suspicion gnawed at Davenport. Something

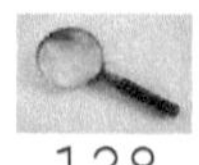

about the brushstrokes, the subtle nuances, felt...off.

The case plunged Moe into the clandestine world of street art, a realm of hidden identities, cryptic messages, and social commentary painted on walls. He delved into the history of Banksy, studying his signature style, his preferred mediums, and the cryptic messages woven into his work. He interviewed other street artists, some wary of outsiders, others eager to share their knowledge of the elusive figure.

Days turned into a blur of dead ends and cryptic clues. Frustration mounted, the pressure from Davenport a constant weight. Just as Moe was about to throw in the towel, a chance encounter at a local art gallery sparked a connection.

A young woman with vibrant hair and paint-splattered overalls spoke of a new artist who had recently emerged in the

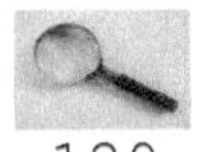

underground scene. This artist, known only as "Enigma," possessed an uncanny ability to mimic the styles of established artists, including Banksy. Her work, while technically masterful, lacked the raw energy and social commentary that defined Banksy's true art.

The pieces clicked into place. Enigma, a talented forger fueled by a desire for recognition, had created the fake Banksy masterpiece. Armed with this information, Moe devised a plan - a daring scheme that would expose the forgery and elevate Enigma's true talent. He contacted a prominent street art festival organizer, convincing him to host a live competition between established artists and a mysterious newcomer - Enigma. The news spread like wildfire, anticipation buzzing through the city's artistic underground.

On the night of the competition, a stage was set up in a trendy downtown venue. Artists, both renowned and anonymous, showcased their talents, the energy electric. Finally, it was Enigma's turn. Wearing a hooded cloak, she stepped onto the stage, her face hidden in shadow.

With a practiced hand, she began to paint. But instead of mimicking Banksy's style, she unleashed her own voice. Her mural depicted a powerful image of social injustice, a commentary on the very system that had sought to silence her. The crowd erupted in cheers, the raw emotion and undeniable talent shining through.

Davenport, initially skeptical, watched with rapt attention. He admitted his mistake, his face a mixture of relief and newfound respect. Enigma, her identity still a secret, became an overnight sensation, her fame built not on forgery,

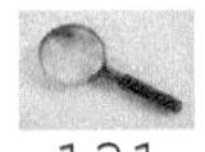

but on the power of her own artistic voice.

As the city lights twinkled outside his window that night, Moe reflected on the day's events. He wasn't just a private investigator; he was a champion for the underdog, a facilitator of second chances, and a weaver of unexpected triumphs in the bustling tapestry of East L.A. life. The whirring fan continued its monotonous song, but a new melody hummed in Moe "Snake Eyes" Juarez's heart - the quiet satisfaction of a job well done, a reminder that even in the heart of a concrete jungle, there was always room for artistic expression and the power of a voice finally heard.

Miguelito Has Disappeared!

A single fan stirred the tepid air, scattering papers across his cluttered

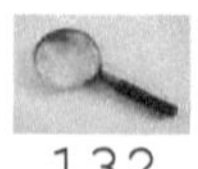

desk. Rent was due, and the only thing fatter than the stack of unpaid bills was his client, Mrs. Hernandez.

"Señor Juarez," she wheezed, her ample bosom straining against a floral print dress, "you must find my Miguelito! He's been gone two days, vanished like a puff of smoke!"

Moe stifled a sigh. Runaway teenagers were a dime a dozen on these dusty streets. But Mrs. Hernandez's tear-filled eyes held a desperation that tugged at him. Besides, her husband, a prominent bakery owner, was rumored to keep a hefty wad of cash on hand.

"Alright, Mrs. Hernandez," Moe said, his voice gravelly from years of cheap cigarettes and strong coffee. "Tell me everything you know."

The story unfolded like a bad telenovela. Miguelito, the golden child, had fallen in with a "no good" crowd - pachinko

parlors and gambling dens that had sprung up since the war. She suspected he was mixed up with something more nefarious, perhaps even kidnapped!

Moe, with his hooded eyes and perpetually suspicious gaze, wasn't buying the kidnapping story. Miguelito was probably holed up somewhere, chasing a cheap thrill and a fast buck. The criminal underworld of East L.A. wasn't known for its hospitality, especially to teenagers with loose lips.

His first stop was the House of Jade, a gambling den Moe knew all too well. The smoky interior reeked of stale beer and desperation. The proprietor, a greasy-haired man named Frankie "The Chin" Molinary, greeted him with a sneer. Frankie wasn't a fan of private investigators, especially ones with a past like Moe's.

"Looking for someone, Snake-Eyes?" Frankie rasped, a gold tooth glinting in the dim light.

"Just asking around," Moe said, his voice a low rumble. He knew Frankie wouldn't budge easily. He tossed a crumpled bill on the bar. "Seen Miguelito Hernandez lately?"

Frankie studied the bill, then Moe. A slow smile spread across his face. "Maybe I have, maybe I haven't. What's it worth to you?"

Moe knew the game. He tossed another bill on the counter. The information came in bits and pieces - Miguelito had been seen around a shuttered warehouse down by the docks. He was with a crew known as "The Aces," a bunch of petty thugs who ran protection rackets for the local numbers games.

The warehouse loomed over the docks, a skeletal silhouette against the blood-

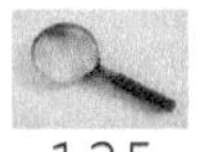

red sky. Inside, the air hung heavy with the smell of mildew and something metallic. Moe crept through the shadows, his hand instinctively reaching for the blackjack he kept holstered under his arm. He found Miguelito huddled in a corner, surrounded by a group of shifty-looking characters.

"Miguelito?" Moe's voice startled the group.

The teenager looked up, his face pale and drawn. Relief warred with defiance in his eyes. Before Moe could intervene, the leader of the Aces, a skinny kid with a switchblade strapped to his arm, stepped forward.

"This ain't your concern, old man," he snarled.

"The Hernandez family is willing to pay," Moe said, his voice hard. He wasn't above a little theatrics.

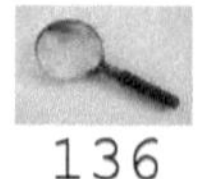

A tense silence followed. Finally, the leader of the Aces scoffed. "Five grand. And you get him outta here."
It was a hefty sum, but Moe knew better than to argue. He relayed the message back to Mrs. Hernandez, who fainted dead away upon hearing the price. Moe rolled his eyes. Some cases never went as planned. But later that night, as Miguelito, sheepish and shaken, was tearfully reunited with his hysterical mother, a flicker of satisfaction warmed the cynical corners of Moe "Snake-Eyes" Juarez's heart. Maybe going straight wasn't so bad after all.

The Jazz Man is Missing

The smog hung thick over East Los Angeles, a greasy film clinging to everything, even Moe "Snake-Eyes" Juarez's office window. The time wasn't

treating the down-on-his-luck private investigator any kinder. Years after his arrest for cheating at that El Monte poker den, the regret still gnawed at him. Back then, a fast hand and a sharper mind kept him afloat. Now, a limp from a bar fight and a reputation that preceded him limited his clientele.

A knock on his door, more of a hesitant tap, startled him. A young woman stood there, her face pale beneath a cheap cloche hat. Her dress, once vibrant green, was now a shade duller, mirroring Moe's own faded glory.

"Mr. Juarez?"

Her voice was barely above a whisper. Moe recognized fear in her wide eyes, the same fear that had mirrored his own back in the joint.

"Come in, miss," he rasped, gesturing to the lone chair in front of his cluttered desk.

She introduced herself as Evelyn Wright,
her husband, a struggling jazz musician
named Tommy, missing for three days.
Panic choked her voice as she spoke of
whispered threats, a gritty bar that
Tommy frequented, and a shady character
known only as "Luckys".

Moe knew Lucky. A two-bit hood with a
penchant for collecting unpaid debts,
often with fists the size of grapefruits.
This wasn't a missing person's case, it
reeked of something more sinister.

Curiosity, a vice as old as time, stirred
within Moe. He wasn't built for heroics
anymore, but something about Evelyn's
trembling hands and the worry etched on
her face tugged at him. Maybe it was a
chance to use his old skills for
something other than staying afloat.

"Alright, Mrs. Wright," he said, his
voice gruff but strangely comforting.
"Let's find your husband."

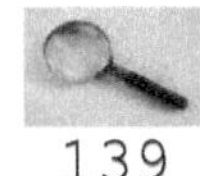

The next few days were a blur of smoke-filled jazz clubs, backroom deals, and whispered threats. Moe navigated the city's underbelly with the ease of a shark in his element. He questioned seedy bartenders, bribed crooked cops with cigarettes, and all the while, the image of Evelyn's tear-streaked face kept him going.

Finally, a lead: Lucky Luciano's warehouse down by the docks. The place reeked of cheap whiskey and desperation. Moe, using his past connections, weaseled his way inside.

He found Tommy, bruised and battered, but alive. A fight gone wrong a debt owed to Lucky. Threats, a beating, the whole sordid story. Just as Moe was about to leave with Tommy, a commotion erupted at the front door.

Police, tipped off anonymously, swarmed the warehouse. Lucky, cornered, pulled a

gun. A shot rang out, echoing through the cavernous space. In the ensuing chaos, Moe hustled Tommy out a back door, the sirens wailing a victory song in the distance.

Back in his office, bandaging Tommy's wounds a small, crumpled bill appeared on the desk. It was ten dollars, the kind of fee that wouldn't even buy a decent bottle of rye. But as Evelyn wrapped her arms around a tearful Tommy, a strange warmth spread through Moe. Maybe being a private investigator in this dirty city wasn't all bad. Maybe, just maybe, he could use his past to help those caught in the same web he once spun.

The sun dipped below the horizon, painting the smog-choked sky in hues of orange and purple. Moe "Snake-Eyes" Juarez, ex-con turned PI, looked out the window, a flicker of hope igniting in his cold, reptilian eyes. The night was

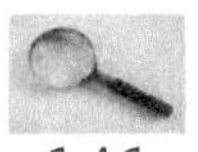

young, and there were more stories waiting to be written in the neon-drenched streets of East Los Angeles.

Watch the Diamonds

The buzz of the city never truly slept, but in the pre-dawn hours, it took on a different rhythm. A lone streetlamp cast an anemic glow on Moe's office door, the only sign of life in the otherwise deserted block.

A guttural cough shattered the quiet. Moe winced, rubbing the sleep from his eyes. A large figure, shrouded in a rumpled trench coat, filled the doorway.

"Snake-Eyes?" The voice was gravelly, laced with a Brooklyn twang.

Moe recognized the accent. East Coast muscle. Trouble with a capital T.

"Depends who's asking," he said, his voice raspy from sleep deprivation.

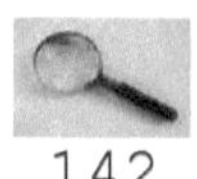

The man stepped into the sliver of light, revealing a face marred by a jagged scar that ran from his temple to his jaw. "The name's Frankie 'Fingers' Falucci. Got a little job for you, if you're interested."

Moe knew the name. Frankie Falucci was a rising star in the L.A. underworld, a brutal enforcer with ambitions that stretched far beyond collecting protection money.

"What kind of job?"

Frankie leaned in, his voice dropping to a conspiratorial whisper. "We got a shipment coming in. Diamonds. Big ones. Need someone to keep an eye on things, make sure it gets from the docks to our warehouse without any mishaps."

Moe's instincts screamed red alert. Getting involved with a high-stakes heist was a recipe for disaster. But the ten-dollar bill from the Wright case still

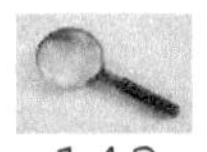

mocked him from the corner of his desk. Besides, a part of him, the part that thrived on the edge, was intrigued.

"What's the cut?" he asked, his voice devoid of emotion.

Frankie smirked, a flash of gold glinting from a chipped tooth. "Five grand. Up front."

The sum was tempting, more money than Moe had seen in a long time. But the risk…

He steepled his fingers, his eyes narrowed. "Alright, Falucci, tell me more."

And so began Moe's descent into the dark underbelly of a city on the cusp of a new decade. The diamond heist, a meticulously planned operation, felt like a step back in time, a return to the days of fast money and quick escapes. Yet, a nagging sense of unease gnawed at him.

Frankie Falucci, for all his bravado, seemed a pawn in a larger game. There

were whispers of rival gangs, double-crosses, and a mysterious figure known only as "The Duchess," a woman rumored to wield power in the shadows.

As the day of the heist approached the air crackled with tension. Moe found himself questioning his loyalties. Was he working for Frankie, or was Frankie just another piece on a chessboard controlled by an unseen hand?

The answer came on a moonless night, down by the docks. The diamond exchange was a chaotic ballet of violence and betrayal. Frankie's men were ambushed, the diamonds vanished, and Moe found himself staring down the barrel of a gun, held not by a rival gang member, but by Frankie himself.

"Seems you played us both, Snake-Eyes," Frankie sneered, his voice laced with venom.

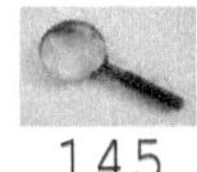

But before he could pull the trigger, a figure emerged from the shadows. The Duchess. Tall, clad in a shimmering emerald dress, on her lips a cruel smile. "Falucci," she purred, her voice smooth as silk, "you've outlived your usefulness."

A single gunshot echoed through the night. Frankie crumpled to the ground his eyes wide with betrayal.

The Duchess turned to Moe, her smile widening. "You, however, seem to have a knack for surviving. Perhaps we can come to an arrangement, Mr. Juarez."

Moe, caught between a rock and a hard place, found himself drawn deeper into the city's underbelly, a reluctant player in a game far more dangerous than he ever imagined. The five grand that had seemed so tempting now felt like a fool's bargain.

The sun peeked over the horizon, painting the sky with streaks of pink and orange. As the city stirred awake, Moe "Snake-Eyes" Juarez, ex-con turned PI, knew his troubles were far from over. The neon lights of East Los Angeles gleamed, a promise of danger and intrigue, and Moe, with a sigh stepped back into the game. The harsh clang of a jail cell door echoed in Moe's ears, jolting him back to reality. The Duchess, it seemed, wasn't a woman of empty threats. He found himself crammed into a stifling cell, the humid air thick with the stench of sweat and despair. His head pounded, a souvenir from a well-placed nightstick courtesy of the Duchess' muscle.

Days bled into nights, measured by the meager meals shoved through a slot in the door. Isolation gnawed at him, his mind a kaleidoscope of memories and regrets. He revisited El Monte, the sting of his

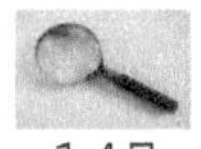

147

arrest, the years wasted behind bars. He
saw Evelyn Wright's tearful face, a stark
reminder of the good he'd almost managed
to do.

One particularly bleak afternoon, the
cell door creaked open. A figure emerged
from the gloom, casting a long shadow
across the grimy floor. It wasn't a
guard, but a man in a crisp suit, a fedora
pulled low over his eyes.

"Mr. Juarez," the man drawled, his voice
clipped and polished. "I believe we have
a proposition for you."

Moe squinted, suspicion hardening his
features. "Who are you?"

The man chuckled, a dry, humorless sound.
"Let's just say I represent certain
interests. Interests that don't
appreciate Ms. Duchess' growing
influence."

He tossed a crumpled photograph onto the
floor. It depicted the Duchess, her face

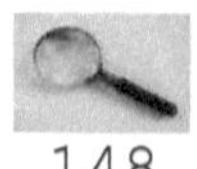

radiating a chilling confidence, flanked by two burly men. One of them, Moe recognized with a jolt, was Frankie Falucci's right-hand man, Fingers.

"She's consolidating power," the man continued. "The diamond heist was just the beginning. We need someone on the inside, someone with her trust."

Moe scoffed. "You think I'd work for another snake like her?"

"We're offering a way out, Mr. Juarez. A chance to clear your name, and a hefty sum to sweeten the deal."

Moe's mind raced. Freedom. A chance to shed the label of ex-con. But trust didn't come easy in this city, and the Duchess wasn't a woman easily fooled.

"What's the catch?"

The man leaned closer, his voice dropping to a conspiratorial whisper. "She's planning a bigger move. A shipment of military-grade weaponry. Enough to tip

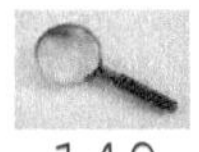

the scales in the ongoing gang war. We
need you to get close, find out where
she's stashing it, and tip us off."
Moe weighed the offer. The potential for
bloodshed, for a whole new war to engulf
the city, sent a shiver down his spine.
But the thought of staying in this cell,
a pawn in someone else's game, was even
more unbearable.
"Alright," he finally said, his voice
rough with disuse. "Get me out of here."
The following days were a blur of
interrogation, threats, and elaborate
conditioning. They drilled him on the
Duchess' known associates, her habits,
her weaknesses. The man in the fedora,
who introduced himself as Mr. Thorne,
became Moe's reluctant mentor.
Finally, the day arrived. Moe, released
from jail with a fabricated story about
a mistaken arrest, found himself walking
free, a caged bird released back into the

jungle. He rented a dingy apartment in a part of town where shadows seemed to linger longer.

Using his old connections, he weaseled his way back into the underground scene. He frequented the bars and gambling dens frequented by the Duchess' men, playing the part of the down-on-his-luck ex-con. He spun elaborate tales of a grudge against Falucci, tales that garnered him a grudging acceptance amongst the Duchess' fringe associates.

It was a slow, dangerous game. Every move felt like a tightrope walk, one wrong step leading to a watery grave at the bottom of the harbor. He cultivated a relationship with Fingers, the scar-faced enforcer, playing the desperate gambler willing to do anything for a chance to win back his losses.

Slowly, painstakingly, the pieces began to fall into place. He learned of a new

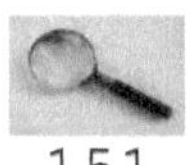

shipment, one arriving under the cover of a phony liquor delivery. The destination, however, remained a mystery.

One particularly raucous night at a smoky jazz club, as the gin loosened tongues and inhibitions, Moe overheard a conversation between Fingers and a hulking brute nicknamed "Bulldog." They spoke of a warehouse on the outskirts of the city, a place guarded like Fort Knox. Hope flickered within Moe. He had his intel.

The weight of the information sat heavy in Moe's gut. He knew finding the Duchess' warehouse was one thing, getting out alive with proof was another. He contacted Mr. Thorne, the voice on the other end a low murmur. "We received your tip," Mr. Thorne said. "The warehouse is our priority. Getting out well, that's up to you, Mr. Juarez."

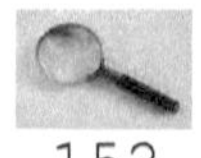

Disappointment gnawed at Moe. He'd been hoping for more, a backup plan, anything. "I need something," he rasped. "A distraction, a way to create a window."

Mr. Thorne chuckled a sound devoid of humor. "We can't exactly call in the cavalry, Mr. Juarez. But let's say there's a rival gang, the Vipers, particularly interested in disrupting the Duchess' operations. A well-placed whisper in their ear could create the chaos you need."

Planting a seed of discord was dangerous, potentially setting off a city-wide war. But Moe saw no other option. He contacted his old barfly friend, a man known as "Leaky Lou" for his inability to keep secrets. Lou's watering hole was a haven for down-and-outers and petty thieves, a perfect breeding ground for rumors.

A few strategically placed drinks later, the story of the Duchess' impending

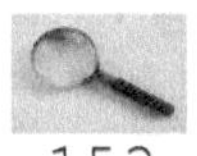

shipment was spreading like wildfire. Lou, fueled by cheap gin and a healthy dose of self-importance, embellished the details, turning a shipment of weaponry into a rumored cache of priceless artifacts.

The next few days were a tense waiting game. The city buzzed with anticipation, the Vipers stirring restlessly. Moe found himself caught in the crossfire, his actions potentially unleashing a storm he couldn't control.

Then came the night. A full moon hung heavy in the sky, casting the city in an eerie silver light. Moe, disguised in a worn dockworker's uniform, slipped into the bustling harbor. His contact, a grizzled longshoreman named "Salty," pointed him towards the warehouse. It loomed on the outskirts, an imposing silhouette against the pale moonlight.

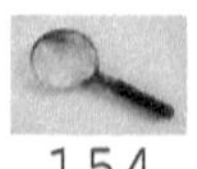

As planned, the warehouse was a scene of chaos. Viper thugs, armed with crowbars and a misguided sense of bravado, clashed with the Duchess' heavily armed guards. The night echoed with gunshots and shouts, a symphony of violence.

Moe snuck through a back entrance, the stench of diesel fuel and sweat clinging to the air. He navigated a maze of crates, his heart hammering a frantic rhythm against his ribs. Every creak, every groan of the building sent chills down his spine.

Finally, he stumbled upon a room guarded by two hulking men. Inside, crates stacked high confirmed his suspicions. This was it. He knew he had seconds, maybe a minute at most, before the chaos outside drew their attention. He fumbled for his camera a small, inconspicuous device provided by Mr. Thorne.

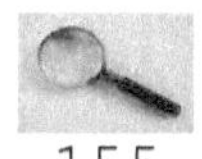

Just as he snapped a picture of the crates' contents, a shadow fell over him. One of the guards, alerted by the click of the camera, spun around, a sneer twisting his features.

"Intruder!" he roared, reaching for his gun.

Time warped for Moe. Fear, cold and sharp, gripped his chest. He lunged for the man, knocking the gun aside. A struggle ensued, a desperate dance of limbs and grunts. In the ensuing chaos, a stray bullet from the fight outside ripped through the window, striking the other guard.

The surviving guard yelled, but before he could fire again, Moe grabbed a nearby crowbar and swung it with all his might. The impact connected with a sickening crunch, sending the guard sprawling.

Panting, adrenaline coursing through his veins, Moe grabbed a second picture of

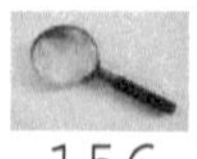

the room, capturing the wounded guard and the incriminating crates. He knew he wouldn't last much longer. The fight outside was winding down, and reinforcements were sure to arrive soon. He sprinted through the warehouse, bullets whizzing past him like angry bees. He reached the back entrance just as a group of Duchess' men, led by Fingers, burst into the room. Confusion clouded their faces as they saw the carnage.

Taking advantage of their momentary disarray, Moe used the chaos to escape back into the night. He melted into the shadows of the docks, the sounds of the waning fight fading behind him.

Reaching a prearranged location, he contacted Mr. Thorne. His voice, breathless with exertion, reported the success of the mission. Mr. Thorne's voice, devoid of emotion, simply

acknowledged the information and instructed Moe to lay low.

He found refuge in a cheap motel room on the outskirts of town, the adrenaline slowly draining away, replaced by a bone-deep weariness. He looked at the small camera, a symbol of his precarious victory.

The following days crawled by in a tense limbo. Moe holed himself up in the cramped motel room, the flickering neon sign outside casting an unwelcome red glow on the peeling wallpaper. The silence was broken only by the insistent buzzing of flies and the occasional wail of a police siren in the distance. He replayed the events at the warehouse over and over, the close calls, the desperate fight. Sleep, when it came, was filled with nightmares of gunshots and sneering faces.

In the morning, a sharp knock on the door shattered the oppressive silence. Steeling his nerves, Moe reached for the gun he'd stashed beneath the threadbare pillow. He wasn't expecting Mr. Thorne, but considering the recent events, caution was paramount.

Cautiously, he cracked open the door a sliver. Standing outside was a young woman, her face framed by a cloud of dark curls. Her emerald green eyes widened as she met Moe's gaze.

"Mr. Juarez?" she asked, her voice barely above a whisper. "It's Evelyn Wright. From Tommy."

His heart stuttered. Evelyn Wright, the woman whose case had lured him back into the dangerous world of private investigation. Memories flooded back - her fear, Tommy's desperation, the smoky haze of the jazz club.

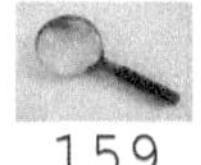

"Evelyn?" he stammered, disbelief coloring his voice. "What are you doing here?"

She stepped back, her gaze flickering nervously down the hallway. "It's not safe here. Can I come in?"

Hesitantly, Moe ushered her inside. The stale air of the room seemed to suffocate them both. Evelyn perched on the edge of the bed, her hands twisting in her lap.

"Tommy's missing again," she blurted out, her voice tight with worry. "He said something about a job for the Duchess, something big. He hasn't been home in two days."

The news slammed into Moe like a physical blow. The Duchess. It couldn't be a coincidence. His gamble, the chaos at the warehouse - had it somehow entangled Tommy?

"Has she contacted you?" he asked, his voice a low growl.

Evelyn shook her head, tears welling up in her eyes. "No, nothing. Just rumors from the neighborhood, whispers about the Duchess and some big operation."

The pieces clicked into place in Moe's mind. Tommy, desperate and out of his depth, most likely had been used as muscle by the Duchess in the aftermath of the Viper raid. Now, with the heat on, she was keeping him out of sight.

"Don't worry, Evelyn," he said, his voice surprisingly steady despite the churning fear in his gut. "I'll find your husband."

There was a flicker of hope in her eyes, but it was quickly replaced by a flicker of something else - knowing. "You're in trouble, aren't you, Mr. Juarez?" she asked, her voice barely a whisper.

Moe couldn't lie to her. He explained his deal with Mr. Thorne, the stolen photographs, the precarious position he

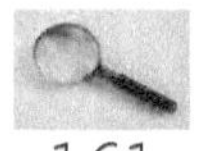

161

was in. Evelyn listened her face etched with concern.

"I can help," she said, surprising him. "Tommy used to play for a joint owned by a man called Dutch. Dutch knows everyone, everyone with a pulse in this city. He might know where Tommy is."

Dutch's bar, a notorious haven for gangsters and down-and-outers, was the last place Moe wanted to go. But with few options left, he had no choice.

That night, under the cloak of darkness, Evelyn led him through a labyrinth of alleyways, the stench of rotting garbage clinging to the humid air. Dutch's bar was a smoky den, the air thick with the smell of cheap bourbon and desperation. A jazz band blared in the corner, the mournful notes clashing with the raucous laughter of patrons.

Evelyn introduced him to Dutch, a portly man with a greasy comb-over and a

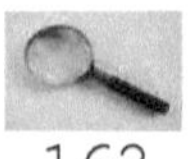

perpetual cigar clamped between his teeth. Dutch eyed Moe with suspicion. "Evelyn tells me you're looking for someone," he rasped, his voice raspy from years of shouting over drunken crowds.

Moe explained Tommy's situation, his voice hoarse with suppressed emotion. Dutch listened, his beady eyes flickering from Moe to Evelyn. He took a long puff of his cigar, the smoke curling up towards the grimy ceiling.

"Tommy was mixed up in somethin' he shouldn't have been," Dutch finally said. "Heard whispers about a shipment, the Duchess movin' some heavy artillery. Seems like Tommy got caught hold of the wrong end of the stick."

He paused, then leaned closer, his voice dropping to a conspiratorial whisper. "Heard they're holed up in an abandoned warehouse near the railroad tracks.

The tip from Dutch sent a jolt through Moe. An abandoned warehouse near the railroad tracks - it was a gamble, but it was their only lead. He thanked Dutch, his stomach churning with a mix of apprehension and a desperate hope.

Back in the stifling motel room, the silence felt oppressive. Evelyn, her face etched with worry, looked at him with pleading eyes.

"We have to help him, Moe," she said, her voice barely a whisper.

Moe knew she was right. Tommy, caught in the crossfire of his own desperation, was likely being used as a pawn by the Duchess. The thought of facing the ruthless gangster queen again sent a shiver down his spine, but the image of Evelyn's tear-streaked face steeled his resolve.

"We'll get him back," he said, his voice gruff but firm. "But we need to be careful. The Duchess doesn't play nice." The next day dawned gray and overcast, mirroring the mood that hung heavy in the air. Following Dutch's cryptic instructions, they navigated a maze of abandoned buildings and overgrown lots, the desolate landscape a stark contrast to the neon-lit chaos of the city center. As they approached the area near the railroad tracks, the air grew thick with the metallic tang of rust and decay. The warehouse, a hulking silhouette against the gloomy sky, looked like a skeletal remnant of a bygone era. Broken windows gaped like empty eyes, and the silence was broken only by the mournful cry of a distant crow.

"Looks deserted," Evelyn whispered her voice barely audible over the pounding of Moe's heart.

He didn't trust appearances. Years on
the streets had taught him that danger
often lurked in the shadows. He crouched
behind a crumbling brick wall, motioning
for Evelyn to stay back. Carefully, he
surveyed the building, his eyes scanning
for any signs of movement.
Nothing. The warehouse seemed abandoned,
a decaying monument to forgotten dreams.
But a nagging unease wouldn't let him
relax. He drew his gun, a relic from his
past life, the familiar weight a cold
comfort in his hand.
With a silent prayer, Moe crept closer,
his senses on high alert. He reached the
entrance, a gaping door swallowed by
darkness. He paused, listening intently.
Not a sound. Taking a deep breath, he
stepped inside.
The air inside was thick with dust motes
dancing in a single shaft of sunlight
filtering through a broken window. The

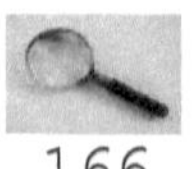

vast space was filled with the skeletal remains of machinery, rusted and abandoned. Silence, thick and oppressive, seemed to press against his eardrums.

He moved cautiously, each creak of the floorboards echoing like a gunshot in the stillness. He explored the ground floor, finding nothing but cobwebs and dust. A metal staircase, its steps groaning under his weight, led him to the second floor. Here, the atmosphere shifted. A faint scent of stale cigarette smoke hung in the air, a jarring contrast to the musty odor below. He followed the trail, his heart hammering a frantic rhythm against his ribs.

The scent led him to a large room, its windows boarded up, plunging the space into an almost complete darkness. A single bare bulb cast an anemic glow on

a makeshift office - a cluttered desk, a chair, and a lone figure slumped over it. As Moe approached, his breath catching in his throat, he recognized the figure. Tommy Wright, his face pale and drawn, slumped unconscious over the desk. Relief washed over Moe like a tidal wave, quickly followed by a surge of anger.

Suddenly, a voice, cold and calculating, sliced through the silence. "Well, well, well. Look who decided to join the party."

Moe spun around his gun raised. Standing in the doorway, bathed in the faint light from the hallway, was the Duchess. She looked even more formidable in person, her emerald green eyes glinting like a predator sizing up its prey.

"Let him go," Moe growled, his voice strained.

The Duchess chuckled a sound devoid of humor. "Ah, Mr. Juarez. Always the

hero. It seems you've been a busy bee, causing quite a stir with your little camera trick."

Moe didn't respond. His eyes darted around the room, searching for an escape route, but there was none. He was trapped, like a fly caught in a spider's web.

The Duchess sauntered into the room, her high heels clicking ominously on the concrete floor. She stopped in front of Tommy, her lips curling into a cruel smile.

"Seems your little musician friend has a talent for getting into trouble," she purred, poking Tommy's shoulder with a manicured nail

Fury surged through Moe. He tightened his grip on the gun, his finger hovering over the trigger. Backing down wasn't an option. He wouldn't let the Duchess intimidate him.

"Leave him out of this," he growled, the words laced with desperation. "This is between you and me."

The Duchess's smile widened, revealing a chilling glint in her eyes. "Always so dramatic, Mr. Juarez. But tell me, what exactly are you proposing? A duel? In this dusty warehouse?"

Moe knew she was toying with him. His mind raced, searching for a way out. He noticed a stack of papers on the desk, partially obscured by Tommy's unconscious form. Perhaps "The pictures," he blurted out. "The ones I took at your warehouse. I have them. If you let Tommy go, I'll give them to you."

The Duchess's smile faltered for a brief moment, a flicker of surprise crossing her face. He saw the gears turning in her head, the calculation of risk and reward.

"And what exactly would I do with blurry photographs?" she countered her voice laced with disbelief. "The authorities wouldn't dare touch someone of my influence."

Moe knew she was right. But desperation fueled him. "Maybe not," he admitted, "but they could cause you trouble. Enemies, rivals — someone would be interested in what you're up to."

A long, tense silence filled the room. Evelyn, hidden in the shadows behind Moe, held her breath. The air crackled with unspoken threats.

Finally, the Duchess broke the silence. She let out a long sigh, a sound of weary resignation. "Fine, Mr. Juarez. You win this time."

She snapped her fingers, and a hulking figure emerged from the shadows. It was Fingers, his face a mask of anger. He

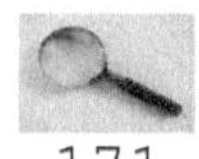

grabbed Tommy, hoisting him over his shoulder like a ragdoll.

"Take him to the car," the Duchess ordered, her voice devoid of emotion.

Fingers grunted in acknowledgment and disappeared back into the darkness.

Relief washed over Moe, but it was short-lived. He knew this wasn't over. The Duchess wasn't one to forgive easily.

"As for you, Mr. Juarez," the Duchess continued, her gaze turning steely, "consider this a warning. Don't get in my way again."

She turned to leave, then paused at the doorway, a hint of a smile playing on her lips.

"And do tell Mr. Thorne "She added, her voice dripping with venom, "that the game is far from over."

With that, the Duchess vanished into the shadows, leaving Moe alone in the dim warehouse with the taste of ashes in his

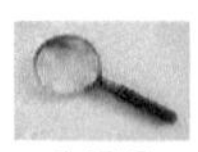

mouth. He lowered his gun, his hand trembling slightly. He had saved Tommy, but at what cost?

Evelyn emerged from her hiding place, rushing to his side. She threw her arms around him, tears streaming down her face.

"Thank you, Moe," she whispered, her voice thick with emotion. "You saved him."

Moe held her close, the weight of the situation pressing down on him. He had won this battle, but the war with the Duchess had just begun. And Mr. Thorne, the enigmatic figure who had pulled him back into this tangled web - he remained a wildcard, his true motives shrouded in mystery.

As they hurried out of the abandoned warehouse, the setting sun cast long shadows across the desolate landscape. The city lights twinkled in the distance,

a beacon of chaos and intrigue. Moe knew he wouldn't be able to walk away from this. The seed of doubt planted by Mr. Thorne had taken root. He needed answers, not just for himself, but for the city that held him captive, a city drowning in its own darkness.

The fight against the Duchess, against the city's underbelly, had become his burden to bear. He was "Snake-Eyes" Juarez, the ex-con turned PI, and this was his twisted sense of redemption. The game was far from over, and Moe, with a steely glint in his cold, reptilian eyes, was ready to play.

Days turned into weeks, the oppressive summer heat clinging to East Los Angeles like a second skin. Moe found himself back in his dingy apartment, a ghost haunting his own life. He'd delivered the stolen photographs to Mr. Thorne through an elaborate network of dead

drops and coded messages. The only
response was a chilling silence, a vacuum
that gnawed at Moe's already frayed
nerves.

Evelyn and Tommy, safe for now, had
relocated to a quiet neighborhood on the
fringes of the city. Moe kept his
distance, a ghost from a past they were
desperately trying to forget. The guilt
gnawed at him. He'd saved Tommy, but at
what cost? He'd drawn Evelyn and her
family into his dangerous world, a world
with consequences he couldn't fully
grasp.

Ernesto is Cheating

It was a sweltering August afternoon when
the latest client came through Moe's
door. She was a young woman named Lupe,
dressed conservatively but with an air of
desperation. She wrung her hands as she

175

took a seat across from Moe's battered desk.

"Please, Mr. Juarez, you have to help me," Lupe pleaded. "My husband Ernesto I think he may be having an affair. He's been coming home late, with flimsy excuses. And there was a strange lady's perfume on his shirt the other night."

Moe nodded wearily. He'd handled his fair share of spouse-trailing jobs over the years. "Don't you fret, Miss Lupe. Ol' Snake-Eyes will get to the truth."

Over the next couple nights, Moe took up a watchful position surveilling Ernesto's movements. He tracked the man from the downtown bodega where he worked to a dim-lit cantina in the barrio. Sure enough, Ernesto met up with an attractive younger woman, and the two slipped out the back entrance together, hands roving intimately.

With a weary sigh, Moe gathered the photographic evidence and took it to Lupe. The poor woman dissolved into heartbroken tears. Case solved, but no joy in delivering that bad news.

The Gang Bangers

Sure enough, his next case came knocking a few nights later. It was an anxious young mother named Rosa who visited his office. Her eyes were hollow from sleepless nights, face etched with worry lines.

"Mr. Juarez, you have to find my son," Rosa pleaded in a trembling voice. "Julio...he got mixed up with a bad crowd, started running with those leather gangs down on Brooklyn Avenue."

Moe leaned forward, features shadowed. "What happened to him, Miss Rosa?"

"Two nights ago, there was a terrible rumble between Julio's gang and their

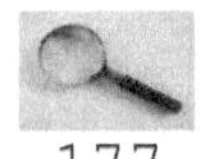

rivals," Rosa went on. "Gunshots, screaming...when it was over, Julio had vanished. The police say maybe he was just scared and laying low, but a mother knows..." She trailed off, wringing her hands.

"You think he got grabbed up by the other crew," Moe said knowingly. "Don't fret, ma'am. Ol' Snake-Eyes will shake the tree and see what falls out."

Over the next couple days, Moe hit the streets hard, calling in every favor and leaning on his shadiest contacts. He eventually tracked down a low-level banger who reluctantly spilled what he knew: Julio had indeed been snatched by the rivals after the bloody fight. They were holding the kid for ransom, planning to bleed his poor family dry before cutting him loose.

Using that lead, Moe traced the captors to a decrepit auto yard on the wrong side

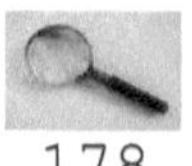

of the tracks. He cased the joint for a couple nights to sort out their numbers and patterns. When the moment was right, Snake-Eyes decided to throw caution to the wind with a headlong assault.

Gunfire erupted in the eerie darkness, muzzle flashes strobing as Moe blasted his way through the startled guards. He could hear Julio's terrified screams from one of the run-down offices as the acrid stench of burnt powder choked the air. The PI stood alone and defiant, barricaded behind an engine block as the gang members tried to regroup and flank him.

That's when the sound of distant sirens began wailing. Moe grinned tightly around the stub of his cigarette - he'd deployed one of the banger's own runners to summon the cops as a backup plan. With the cavalry en route, the gang dissolved into panicked retreat, leaving Moe to scoop up

the battered but relieved Julio and
hustle him to safety.

A few days later, the tearful reunion
between Rosa and her son was one for
Moe's memory books. The grateful mother
swept him up in a bone-crusher hug amid
her sobbing, offering to pay him double
his rate. Moe just shook his head -
seeing families made whole again was
payment enough.

After Rosa and Julio departed, Moe
settled back behind his desk with a fresh
toothpick, already pondering whatever
crisis would come crashing through his
doorway next. Olympic Blvd. threw
curveballs at you every day. But ol'
Snake-Eyes lived for solving those nasty
tangles, protecting the everyday folk who
scratched and scrambled in this crazy
East LA pressure cooker. He was their
watchdog, their shadowy guardian angel
watching over all the dark corners.

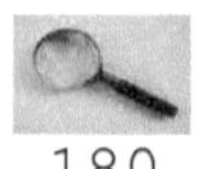

180

To Moe, that was a life worth living.
Even after closing the case of Rosa's missing son Julio, there was little respite for Moe "Snake-Eyes" Juarez in his perpetual vigil over East LA's mean streets.

The Bookies Been Hit

His next client arrived in the boozy pre-dawn hours, pounding desperately on Moe's office door. It was a wild-eyed fellow named Marco, a small-time bookie who ran an illicit gambling setup out of a backroom at El Norteño bar.

Marco burst in gasping shirt drenched with sweat. "Juarez, I need your help, man! They took everything - the entire night's take!"

Moe calmly lit a cigarette, letting the bookie ramble. "You better start making sense, Marco. Took what?"

"The money!" Marco wheezed, throwing up his hands. "We had a huge evening - dogs, horses, you name it. Must've been close to ten grand in the vault. But this morning, it was all gone! Place was busted wide open!"

Moe's eyes narrowed. Ten grand was serious money, even for the heavies in this town. "Who'd you tick off bad enough for a heist like that?"

Marco raked his hands through his thinning hair. "Could've been any of the high-rollers that hit us up! Moretti's guys, the Cohen outfit, the damned Baros brothers and their vato crew!"

This had all the markings of a contracted hit by one of the East L.A. crime families. Trying to sort through Marco's tangled underworld web of debtors and enemies would be a nightmare. But Moe had faced worse headaches - and $10,000 was

a lucrative payout if he could crack this case.

"Aright, aright, saddle up," Moe relented with a sigh. "Show me the scene of this disastrous crime so I can get started sniffing out trails."

What ensued was a typical noir-laced investigation that consumed Moe's days and nights. He ran the muggy gauntlet between Chavez Ravine and Montebello, gathering clues from Marco's gambling associates about who might be gunning for the bookie's operation.

Threats, roughhousing, and very liberal applications of bribery eventually pointed Moe toward an unlikely suspect - Carmela Delgado, the cunning but aging leader of the Barra Brava gang that ran certain quarters of East LA. Apparently Marco had gotten way behind on his compensations to her crew for allowing his bookmaking on their turf.

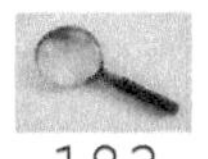

Rattling a few cages finally uncovered what Moe needed to know. He discovered Delgado's gang had carried out the daring robbery of Marco's vault, but the money wasn't their final endgame. They were using the bookie's riches as a piggy bank to finance an ambitious series of hits - all aimed at finally eliminating their hated rivals, the Latino street gang known as White Fence.

With the clock ticking, Moe would have to infiltrate Delgado's fiercely-guarded compound and somehow recover Marco's money before it could spark a full-blown gang war across East LA. This would mean going full Snake-Eyes, employing every lethal trick and hustle he'd learned over the decades...

Moe "Snake-Eyes" Juarez knew infiltrating Carmela Delgado's heavily fortified compound would be a near-suicidal mission. The aged gang leader's

headquarters was a veritable fortress in the heart of her Barra Brava crew's territory. Getting in would be the easy part - making it out alive with Marco's stolen money was another beast entirely.

First, the PI needed to assemble a ragtag team of specialists he could desperately trust. He called in a few favors, gathering a motley group that included a safecracker, a wheelman, and a wiry but vicious brawler who'd grown up throwing fists in the East LA fighting pits.

After a tense planning session downing jugs of Cuban rotgut, they were ready to make their play. Under cover of night, they slipped past the outer security parameters like ghosts. So far, so good - until a roving guard patrol stumbled upon them near Delgado's inner compound. All hell broke loose. Moe's brawler buddy erupted into a whirlwind of crunching blows, silently dropping two of the

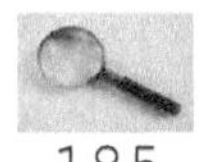

guards before they could raise an alarm. But a third managed to get off a burst of automatic fire that cut the whip-thin fighter down in a splatter of gore.

Cursing, Moe and his safecracker pal Freddie beat feet toward the central armory building where Delgado's stolen cash was reportedly stashed. More of the Barra Brava gang was quickly swarming towards them now, shouts and gunshots reverberating through the night air.

"Get that damned door open!" Moe shouted above the din, snapping off revolver shots to cover Freddie as he worked furiously on the armory's reinforced locks. Within moments, they were tumbling inside and slamming the heavy door shut on their pursuers.

By the guttering light of a kerosene lamp, they spied the prize - an antique metal behemoth of a safe, large enough to hold Marco's entire pilfered haul. But

before Freddie could get to work, a gravelly voice froze them in their tracks.

"I'm impressed you made it this far, Snake-Eyes. But your journey ends here, cabron."

Carmela Delgado stepped from the shadows, cold eyes glinting as she leveled a pearl-handled automatic towards them. Two hulking bodyguards flanked her, slabbed muscles twitching beneath their sweat-stained wife-beaters.

Moe instinctively went for his revolver, but the bodyguards were faster. One brutal pistol-whip laid him out in a haze of bursting stars. As his world grayed, he could see Freddie crumpling as well, leaving them defenseless before the merciless Delgado...

With a grunt of pain, Moe came back to groggy semi-consciousness, his vision blurred and head ringing. He was bound

tightly to a chair, flanked by the two brutish bodyguards while the diminutive but terrifying form of Carmela Delgado loomed before him.

The aged gang leader was languidly puffing on a thin cigarillo, the wispy smoke coiling around her impassive features. "Did you really think it would be so easy to infiltrate my compound, Snake-Eyes?" she asked in a raspy voice. "To steal what is rightfully mine?"

Moe blinked to focus his eyes, realizing with a jolt that poor Freddie the safecracker was also tied up beside him, a massive welt across his bloodied forehead. At least the skinny guy was still breathing.

"Way I heard it...that money don't belong to you, abuela," Moe rasped defiantly. "It's hot, straight from Marco's gambling vaults."

Delgado's eyes flashed with displeasure and she lashed out suddenly, cracking Moe across the face with the heavy pearl grip of her pistol. He could taste the warm copper burst of blood in his mouth.

"Suffer the same arrogance that's crippled so many before you, Snake-Eyes," the ruthless matriarch hissed. "You underestimate my reach, my power." She turned to one of the hovering bodyguards, gesturing dismissively with her cigarillo. "Bring him."

The hulking brute disappeared for a moment, grunts and muffled shouts echoing from a backroom. When he re-emerged, he was dragging a beaten, slurring form that made Moe's gut clench - it was Marco himself, the hapless bookie who'd hired him. He'd been captured as well trying to recover his own money.

"Recognize your employer, detective?" Delgado taunted as Marco was flung beside

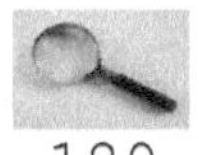

the chairs, groaning. "He was a foolish
enough to believe he could move his
operation onto my streets without
compensating La Barra Brava."
She turned her withering glare back
towards Moe. "His careless arrogance bred
more of the same in you, Snake-Eyes.
You'll all learn the consequences of such
insult."
With a subtle nod, the bodyguards began
beating and kicking the helpless Marco
without mercy, his muffled shrieks
echoing in the dank chamber. Try as he
might, Moe could do nothing but watch in
mute rage as the life was brutalized out
of his unfortunate client.
At last, Delgado raised a hand to halt
the merciless assault, her cronies
stepping back from Marco's motionless,
bloody form. She stepped up to Moe's
chair, pressing the still-hot muzzle of
her pistol under his jaw.

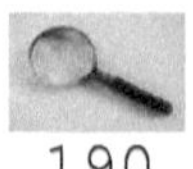

190

"You're next, detective," she snarled, her flinty gaze unwavering. "Unless you have a remarkably compelling reason for me to spare you and your buddy."

Moe stared back at the tiny, hardened criminal matriarch and felt his chances for survival slipping away with each ragged breath. This aging firecracker held all the cards...or did she? Maybe one desperate gambit remained to turn the tables.

With the cold muzzle of Delgado's pistol digging into the soft flesh under his jaw, Moe "Snake-Eyes" Juarez knew his options for survival were rapidly dwindling. All around him were the gang leader's hulking enforcers, ready to unleash more brutal beatings at her whim. His client Marco lay motionless and likely dead on the filthy floor.

He flicked his gaze momentarily to poor Freddie beside him. The wiry little

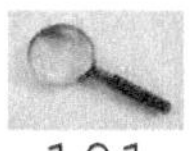

safecracker's eyes were wide with fear, blood oozing from the welt on his forehead. Moe gave him the slightest shake of his head - a warning not to try anything rash and stupid. This wasn't some penny-ante caper gone sideways. They were staring down the barrel of certain death.

Unless Moe could desperately spin one of his trademark cons. Lie, bluff and hustle with all he had to wriggle free of this precarious situation. He'd pulled off such long-shot gambles countless times over his colorful career. Could he muster one more miracle play?

Locking eyes with the diminutive but utterly lethal Delgado, Moe cleared his throat and started in with his silkiest patter.

"Easy there, queen... You know me better than these games. Sure, Marco hired me to go after his scratch. But that was just

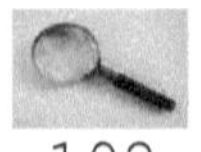

the ritual dance - the real play was always for you and me to go ahead and make a deal."

The pistol wavered slightly as Delgado arched one sculpted eyebrow in faint curiosity. Moe knew he had her attention, for now. He pressed on quickly.

"Way I figured, you'd snatch that money to kick off your big move against White Fence right? Make sense to any veteran of the streets like us. But then it hit me - what you gonna need more than just that starter wad is an angle, a way to get inside their operation. Infiltrate, undermine, really stick a knife in their ambitions to run roughshod over your barrios..."

Delgado's eyes narrowed further, but she stayed silent, allowing Moe to continue spinning his desperate yarn.

"That's where a cagey detective like me finally comes in useful, see?" Moe gave

her his most charming grin, feeling sweat trickle down his back. "You keep me breathing, and I'll be your Insider man with White Fence. Get you those internal details no heavy hand could ever uncover on their own. Lines get blurred, you know I can sidle and slip right through any of their circles without raising any red flags."

The silence stretched on unbearably as Moe finished his gambit, gauging whether his bold lies and half-truths had found just enough plausibility with Delgado. She was as crafty as they came, after all. Finally, she spoke in a low rasp.

"You think you can work me so easily, Snake-Eyes? That I'd entertain such a fool's bargain when your deceptions are plain?"

Moe felt his heart lurch, but refused to let his face betray any hint of defeat.

Poker-faced, he gave a slight shrug of his bound shoulders.

"Seems awfully rash to flush a still-breathing asset down a hole over a little misunderstanding. I ain't got no skin in your upcoming battle, Queen but I could prove mighty useful for infiltrating your enemies no?"

The tense pause stretched out again. From the corner of his eye, Moe could see poor Freddie was trembling, likely envisioning the torrent of violence that could erupt if Delgado didn't take the bait.

Then, almost imperceptibly, Delgado gave the slightest nod and lowered her pistol. Moe felt his spirit's soar, though he refused to show even a flicker of triumph on his impassive features.

"Very well, Snake-Eyes," the gang matriarch said evenly. "Bargain

acceded...for now. Do not make me regret leaving breath in your body."

She spun and strode away, barking orders at her crew to "let the idiotos go" and make preparations. As the bodyguards moved to cut Moe and Freddie's bonds, relief and new worry flowed over the PI in equal measure.

His big mouth had bought them potentially precious time...but could he actually deliver on his audacious bluff about infiltrating the dreaded White Fence gang?

With sweat beading on his brow, Moe "Snake-Eyes" Juarez allowed himself to be untied and hauled to his feet by Delgado's hulking goon squad. His hands were still securely bound, but at least he could breathe freely now without the barrel of a gun jammed under his jaw.

The diminutive but utterly ruthless gang matriarch watched with impassive eyes as

Moe and poor Freddie were frog-marched from the dank armory room where their gambit had played out. She puffed slowly on her thin cigarillo, coils of acrid smoke wafting through the dim light.

"Do not doubt I will revisit your usefulness soon, Snake-Eyes," Delgado warned in her papery rasp. "And if I detect even a whisper of betrayal in your actions..."

She let the threat hang ominously as she pulled Moe close, stinking of cheap tobacco and cruelty. Her diamond-studded rings dug painfully into his bicep.

"I will show you what pure suffering truly is, detective. This will seem like a nursery story by comparison. Am I clear?"

Moe gave a slight nod, jaw clenched tightly. He could hear Freddie whimpering faintly beside him. "Crystal, queen," he managed to grit out.

With that, the bodyguards propelled them out into the sweltering East LA night. Moe squinted against the harsh lights of the Barra Brava compound the rest of the dangerous barrio enveloped in inky shadows all around them. A battered sedan idled nearby, exhaust fumes hanging in the still air.

With none-too-gentle shoves, Moe and Freddie were bundled into the vehicle's backseat. One of the hulking bodyguards slid in beside them, an antique but wicked-looking revolver leveled inches from Moe's face.

"You try any funny business and I'll splash your brain across this upholstery, hear me?" the ruthless Chicano hissed, dark eyes glistening with psychopathic menace.

The PI simply gave a tight nod, unwilling to risk provoking more violence and

ruining the precarious reprieve he'd bought with his silver tongue. For now. The car's engine snarled and they peeled out, burning rubber as the compound fell away behind them. Moe stared grimly ahead through the cracked windshield, his mind racing over the near-disasters of the past few hours - not to mention the incredibly risky road he'd now committed to stumble down next.

Infiltrating White Fence, the most savage gang outfit in all of East LA, to act as a mole for his new "employer" Carmela Delgado? He might as well have accepted a suicide mission written on a marble slab.

Still...Moe had faced outrageous odds and escaped with his life more times than he could count over his long career as a private eye. If anyone could pull off such an insane gambit, it was Snake-Eyes Juarez himself - assuming his faltering

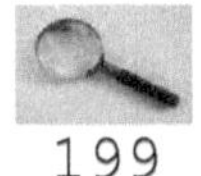

luck hadn't finally run bone-dry in this blast-furnace of a city.

As the battered sedan carried them deeper into the darkness cloaking East LA's most perilous neighborhoods, Moe's mouth settled into a grim line. He was in deep, and they all knew it. But he'd burn that bridge when he came to it.

For now, it was time to figure out how to slither his way into the belly of the snake - the Viper's Nest itself - without ending up Fanged.

Moe "Snake-Eyes" Juarez leaned back in the battered sedan's cracked vinyl seat, hands still bound, and tried to steady his racing mind. He'd just pulled off an incredible gambit, spinning a tale outrageous enough to temporarily spare his life at the hands of the ruthless gang leader Carmela Delgado. But that hustle had come with heavy stakes - he was now expected to infiltrate Delgado's

hated rival gang, White Fence, and feed her intelligence from the inside.

As the vehicle rumbled through East LA's meanest barrios, Moe studied his captors from the corners of his eyes. The two hulking bodyguards flanking him in the backseat looked like they'd been carved out of oak and bad intentions. They gripped antique revolvers, undoubtedly itching for an excuse to ventilate the PI's skull all over the upholstery.

Up front, the wiry but cold-eyed driver guided them with a brutal calm born from years navigating this violent urban geometry. Sporadic muzzle flashes flickered in the distance like heatwave mirages, accompanied by the echoing pop-pop of small arms fire. Just another night in the districts bordering City Terrace and Belvedere.

Beside Moe, poor Freddie was alternating between panicked hyperventilation and

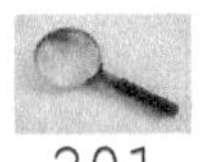

feverish mumbling in Spanish - a little too on-the-nose for the PI's liking right now. With an elbow jab, he hissed "Can it, willya?" at the terrified safecracker under his breath.

The big bodyguard closest to Freddie responded with a vicious backhanded slap that snapped the skinny man's head violently to the side.

"Keep your buddy's mouth zipped, detective," he growled in thickly-accented English. "Before I do it permanent-style for him."

Freddie immediately fell into a cowed, trembling silence. Moe gave a tight nod to indicate he understood, fingers drumming rapidly against his bound wrists. He needed to stay frosty and find a way to ditch this clown act soon. Every mile deeper into White Fence' heavily fortified territories was another length of rope for them to hang themselves with.

They were rapidly closing in on the nightmarishly violent no-man's land of the Eastside Pride housing projects. The driver checked a specific side street then accelerated hard into a tight turn. Instantly, the precision driving turned into a desperate scramble as bullets hammered the sedan's bodywork in a sudden ambush! The driver instinctively ducked down as inch-thick heavy slugs Spider-webbed the windshield and punctured the front quarter panel in a blistering fusillade.

"Ambush! Ambush!" one of the goons shouted unnecessarily, snapping off wild retaliatory fire through the shattered rear windows with his revolver. Moe threw himself across Freddie as the man soiled himself in sheer terror.

Through the chaos of shattering glass and thunder of gunshots, Moe's razor instincts quickly determined they were

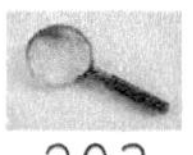

caught in the urban crossfire of a
territorial clash between rival sets. The
driver hauled the battered sedan into a
bone-jarring U-turn and hit the gas,
fishtailing in a spray of bullets that
pursued them like furious wasps for
several blocks.

Finally, Moe felt the unmistakable sense
that they'd blundered across some
invisible borderline to relative Safety,
the gunfire dwindling behind them. He
pulled himself upright, grimacing at the
fresh bloom of blood on his sleeve from
a graze wound. Freddie was pale and
sweating, blessedly uninjured.

The big bodyguards swapped tense looks,
the non-English speaker spitting a long
stream of curses towards the shredded
rear window. Up front, the driver was
doubled over the wheel, sucking frantic
draughts of air between his clenched
teeth.

"Control yourselves, cabrones," the English-speaking heavy snapped. He turned his dead-eyed glare on Moe. "A little spilled blood ain't nothing new for the Barra Brava. Ain't that right, Snake-Eyes?"

Moe gave the slightest nod, trying to conceal the maelstrom of calculations roiling in his brain behind an unflappable facade. He needed to extricate himself and Freddie from this White Fence nest, and fast - before the next strike from the frayed Arañas put them six feet under.

The question was...how?

As the battered sedan careened away from the fresh ambush, Moe "Snake-Eyes" Juarez felt his pulse thundering in his ears. They'd narrowly escaped being caught in the crossfire of an erupting gang war between the Barra Brava and their rivals, White Fence. Bullets had chewed into the

vehicle's bodywork like a buzzsaw through aluminum.

Up front, the driver was visibly shaken, raking trembling hands through his slick hair as he struggled to regain his bearings. In the rearview, Moe could see the hardened man's eyes were wide and dilated, a thin sheen of sweat on his brow.

The two bodyguards flanking the PI and poor Freddie weren't faring much better. The larger one - Moe's personal gun barrel concierge - kept craning his neck to scan the maze of side streets and alleys whipping past. His knuckles were white where he gripped the ancient revolver, prepared for any further ambushes.

Freddie, the wiry little safecracker, alternated between quiet whimpering sobs and sporadic hyperventilating gasps. Moe resisted the urge to shake him, not

wanting to attract undue attention or violence from their increasingly volatile captors.

Instead, the PI forced himself to breathe slowly, automatically cataloging their current surroundings and tactically reassessing with each passing block. They were clearly still deep in hardcore White Fence territory judging by the increasingly decayed urban landscape. Fortified lookout nests lined the rooftops of squat tenement buildings, the chipped facades spraypainted with taunting gang insignias.

Every other storefront was battered and abandoned, some with gaping holes from past fire bombings. Streetlight pools were populated by silent, wary-eyed huddles of lookouts wearing the White Fence colors. They eyed the passing sedan with undisguised disdain and hostility.

To Moe, this entire district resembled the worst demilitarized zone of some war-ravaged third world country. And the maddening reality was - he'd "negotiated" his way into attempting an infiltration of these streets, brimming with heavy gunfire and murderous sectarian grudges thicker than the shimmering summer haze. He flexed his wrists imperceptibly, testing the coarse but unyielding bite of his nylon restraints. Getting free was the first priority. Then figuring out how to ditch these lumbering jokes of "bodyguards" without getting all of their throats cut on a dusty side street. And after that...

After that, the real game would begin. Somehow snaking his way into the inner circles of White Fence, convincing them of his usefulness and protected status without betraying his real identity as a PI. All while feeding intel back to the

snake pit of the Barra Brava in exchange for his life.

Easy, right? Moe's face settled into a stony mask, not betraying the slightest hint of mirth at the sheer insanity of his current predicament. All he had to do was play the role of a lifetime.

Without getting himself and poor Freddie ventilated in an endless cycle of gang retaliation, that was. Just another warm summer evening in the glorious slaughterhouse of East Los Angeles.

The sedan made a hard right onto a slightly wider thoroughfare, momentarily straightening its course. Up ahead, a burned-out civic center loomed from behind walls of coiled razor wire and graffiti-bombed concrete barricades.

This had all the markings of being deeper into White Fence' stranglehold territory. Moe's eyes narrowed as he studied their apparent destination: a

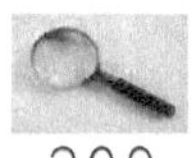

squat, fortress-like building standing in the shadow of the blasted municipal complex.

It appeared to be some sort of heavily-fortified social club or headquarters. The barricades funneled all approaching traffic into a narrow, controlled entry corridor festooned with heavy weaponry and roving patrols. Snake-Eyes recognized the unmistakable silhouette of a .50 caliber machinegun nest glowering from one of the elevated watch positions.

As their vehicle slowed to clear the armed checkpoints, Moe made certain his facade was locked into place - the wary confidence of a cagey street operative, hiding any potential nerves or fear. They were about to enter the viper's den itself. The slightest misstep, sign of weakness or deception could spell instant execution from these ruthless Cholos.

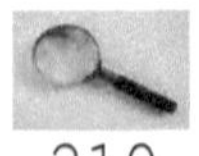

It was make-or-break time for Juarez's latest, most improbable of cons. If he could just keep his cool and maintain the hustle... there was the faintest chance he could survive long enough to turn the tables.

Maybe.

Moe "Snake-Eyes" Juarez held his breath as the battered sedan rolled through the fortified checkpoint and into the heart of White Fences' stronghold. All around them, the unmistakable aura of menace and brutality hung heavy as a burial shroud. Feral-eyed Cholos in White Fence-emblazoned colors prowled the encrusted alleyways, gripping antique but vicious firearms. Some clutched broken bottles, lengths of chain, or wicked-looking clubs fashioned from rebar and spikes. They eyed the passing vehicle with a blend of wariness and unbridled hostility.

On the rooftops, makeshift sniper nests had been cobbled together from ancient sandbags, wooden slats, and salvaged awning materials. The sunbaked urban hellscape exuded a palpable sense that routine and casual violence could erupt at any moment without warning.

Moe felt sweat trickling down his spine as the sedan pulled up to the primary compound - a squat, bunker-like structure bristling with improvised fortifications. It looked like one of those anarchic fiefdoms that emerged during failed insurgencies in the world's most brutal hot zones.

As the vehicle's doors were wrenched open, a fresh wave of humidity and stench washed over them - the ripe, unforgettable odor of squalor, body odor, and slow decay blended into one. It was the unmistakable stench of the damned concentrated in tight, sordid quarters.

212

"Out, cabrones," one of Moe's brutish bodyguard escorts growled, gesturing with the muzzle of his antique revolver. "Welcome to Casa de la White Fence."

Gritting his teeth, Moe complied smoothly, unfolding himself from the sedan's cramped confines with studied nonchalance. He wasn't about to show the slightest weakness before this viper's nest of sociopathic killers.

Freddie, in contrast, practically fell from the vehicle in a gasping, trembling heap. He'd been utterly shell-shocked into catatonia from the earlier ambush and the sights now surrounding them. One heavy-booted kick from the guard sent him scurrying ahead of Moe, head bowed submissively.

They were quickly encircled by a small phalanx of White Fence hardcases, their cold eyes visibly assessing Moe and his unfortunate companion. Scarred,

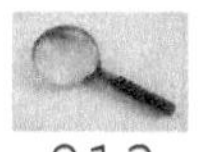

calloused hands rested on machetes, pistol grips, and weighted clubs with a practiced ease that spoke volumes. This was no posturing force - every one of them had clearly dealt out and received countless brutal beatings as part of their daily business.

A sudden commotion rippled through the entrance as a dented wrought-iron door screeched open nearby. Two more towering bruisers emerged flanking a slight but utterly menacing figure drenched in White Fence tattoos and gold jewelry.

Time seemed to slow for Moe as he found himself face-to-face with El Frío himself - legendary leader of White Fence and one of the most dangerous criminals stalking the whole of greater East Los Angeles.

The diminutive but feral-eyed gang boss prowled in a slow circle around Moe and Freddie, lips peeled back in a rictus of cruel amusement. At a subtle hand signal,

his two hulking guardians slammed the cowering safecracker to his knees with rifle butts to the abdomen.

"Snake-Eyes Juarez himself," El Frío rasped in accented English, eyes glittering with dark mirth. "To what do we owe the honor, detective?"

In that moment, Moe felt utterly alone, a tiny spark of life surrounded by a roiling sea of pitiless violence, poverty and decay. This was the dark heart of the East LA badlands, straight from the fever dreams of Dante or Bosch. If he played his hustle wrong here, it wouldn't just spell his demise.

It would mean being erased, utterly and permanently, from all existence. With a monumental force of will, he kept his voice controlled, neutral.

"Just a little detour on my way to someplace, Frío. Not looking to throw

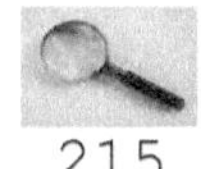

weight around your bailiwick without cutting business first, you dig?"

The vicious gang leader's teeth flashed in something approximating a grin. "Indeed. We should discuss terms then, no?"

As he was prodded ahead of the merciless thug entourage towards whatever circle of hell awaited inside White Fence' heavily-fortified den, Moe somehow suppressed the tremor that wanted to overtake him.

One thing was excruciatingly clear - he'd just entered the most dangerous possible gambit of his checkered career. If he couldn't hustle and con his way out of the viper's nest, it wouldn't just be his own wretched life forfeited before the sun set over this urban apocalypse.

Poor Freddie didn't stand a chance of making it out breathing either.

Moe "Snake-Eyes" Juarez felt his heart thudding in his chest as he was prodded

through the fortified entrance and into the heart of White Fence' brutal stronghold. All around, a seething atmosphere of impoverished squalor and ever-present violence hung like a big stink.

Feral-eyed gang members adorned in White Fence tattoos and gang insignia glared at the newcomers with undisguised hostility. Scarred hands clenched makeshift weapons - machetes, chains, lengths of pipe - in anticipation of any wrong move that could spark sudden bloodshed. It was pure chaos barely constrained within these cracked adobe walls.

At Moe's side, poor Freddie remained a sniveling, trembling wreck after being physically cowed by El Frío's merciless enforcers. The scrawny safecracker's face was already purpling into an impressive shiner from the vicious rifle-

butt strike he'd taken to the gut. Moe realized the odds of them both making it out of this pit alive were becoming increasingly slim.

They were brusquely escorted deeper into White Fence' maze-like patchwork of squat buildings, graffiti-bombed hallways, and impromptu barricades fashioned from blast walls and overturned vehicles. Everywhere Moe turned, there were more cholos lounging about in hardened repose, nursing firearms and bottles of gut-burning alcohol or huffing gasoline fumes to stay endlessly wired.

The PI felt rising unease claw at his nerves as they navigated the gauntlet of abject conditions and feral glares. He was a seasoned survivor of the East LA underworld, but this went beyond even the most blighted corners he'd seen before. At last, they reached the central headquarters of White Fence - a semi-

fortified building that appeared to have once been a small community center or auditorium. Now, it was clearly the nerve center of El Frío's ruthless narco-empire, the wretched living heart pumping lifeblood through this ultra-violent body.

Moe and Freddie were shoved into a dimly-lit central room that reeked of sweat, cigarette smoke, and spilled malt liquor. A series of low wooden benches surrounded a raised dais at one end, where a sinister-looking high-backed chair resembling an extravagant throne held court.

At a subtle hand gesture from the diminutive but utterly vicious El Frío, Moe found himself and Freddie forced to their knees before the sneering gang boss. Frío settled into his gilded throne with an imperious indifference, surveying his visitors like scraggly

street dogs just moments from being put down.

"So, detective," he began casually, "you find yourself most unexpectedly in our casa. I would be negligent if I did not inquire into your motivations for gracing us with your renowned presence, no?"

Moe clenched his jaw to stop it from visibly quivering. Every instinct was screaming at him to divert, deflect, do anything but reveal his true hand - a hand that, at the moment, he wasn't even fully holding himself. El Frío was clearly unconvinced Moe was any kind of player or operator worth tolerating alive within his sadistic little kingdom.

The PI would need to hustle like his life utterly depended on it...because in that tiny, smoke-choked audience chamber, it absolutely did.

Casting a furtive glance at the still-cowering Freddie, Moe cleared his throat.

220

"Look, Frío I ain't here to throw heat and disrespect around, you dig? Not looking to step on any toes and get nerds flaring."

Moe could almost see the depraved wheels turning behind those dark sockets as he pressed on.

"Way I hear it, you got your own flaming slap down in progress with that Barra Brava set, am I right?" Frío gave the slightest inclination of a nod, allowing Moe to continue spinning his desperate tale.

"Well, I got a connect from deep inside Carmela's whole operation who figured a smart vato like myself might want a piece of that sweet action..."

Moe could feel the temperature in the smoke-choked chamber seem to drop several degrees as every hardened gangster present locked their feral gazes directly onto him. He was treading on extremely

thin ice here, attempting to bluff his way into portraying himself as a deep-cover asset against the Barra Brava - White Fence' most hated rivals.

Any slight misstep, any waver in his conviction or faltering of his story could spell instant erasure. These narco-savages would shed his and Freddie's blood without a second thought.

Keeping his expression neutral, Moe pressed on boldly. "Word was Carmela caught wind of your set making a play to muscle in on her beloved East L.A. territories. She's scared, scared enough to put some insurance on the streets."

The deafening silence hung in the room like a vise around Moe's throat. Was this insane gambit even registering as plausible? Or could El Frío's merciless gaze see straight through to the truth - that Moe was just an overmatched PI in way over his head?

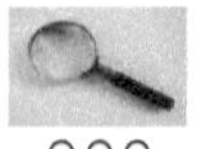

Then, the slightest ghost of a cruel smile played across the vicious gang leader's lips. He leaned forward in his baroque throne, elbows on the rests.

"You claim to be some deep ramen from within La Barra's very heart, eh Snake-Eyes?" His tone dripped with sardonic amusement. "Some embedded Judas eager to feed us intel on the movements of Carmela Delgado herself?"

Moe gave a slight dip of his chin in affirmation, hoping his poker face remained inscrutable. Inside, his guts were liquid ice water threatening to betray his desperation.

The cruel smirk intensified minutely. "We will see..." El Frío murmured, eyes glittering like a reptile's.

With a subtle hand gesture, two of the gang leader's hulking bodyguards moved to flank Moe and poor Freddie. In one brutal moment, they were wrenched to their feet,

the guards' calloused hands closing like savage vice grips around their throats. Moe felt the sudden burn of fatigue poison in his body as his airway was instantly cut off. Beside him, Freddie's bulging eyes rolled back in his skull as he started to turn an alarming shade of purple. The PI frantically tried to rasp out some form of protest or deal, but only feeble wheezes emerged.

El Frío leaned back again, an insouciant monarch watching his sport. His voice was almost inaudible over the harsh, desperate sounds of strangled respiration echoing through the chamber. With a subtle nod, the bodyguard's grips relaxed a mere fraction for Moe and Freddie, allowing precious airflow.

"But...perhaps there could be some benefit in having one of Delgado's own allowed to roam freely, no? Feeding us with her foul secrets, comprende?"

Chest heaving, Moe gave a mute nod of comprehension as he gulped air back into his rebelling lungs. This was what he'd been gambling everything on - his raw persuasive skills and ability to stay ahead of El Frío's sadistic windings. For now, the vicious gang lord was intrigued enough by Moe's Barra Brava mole story to keep the pair breathing.

The only question was how long such a risky bluff could persist before El Frío decided to extract the truth in more visceral ways. And if that happened, Moe and Freddie wouldn't just be snuffed out their suffering would be incendiary.

As he started to regain his senses, daring to hope he'd slipped the noose for the moment, Moe noticed an odd detail on El Frío's left hand. Glinting unmistakably beneath the tatted flesh and gold rings was a distinctive wristwatch - a high-end, centuries-old piece that

looked massively out of place adorning this avatar of human cruelty.

His mind raced as the gang leader continued extolling on the potential "values" Moe's phantom undercover status could bring to the White Fence gang. What was the story behind that opulent watch? Some twisted trophy claimed in blood and savagery?

Or could it possibly be...a vital clue Moe had been missing in his increasingly labyrinthine quest to escape this urban maze of violent terror with his life intact?

There was only one way to find out. All the PI could do was keep his wits, play his role to the hilt, and pray his hustling skills were still as sharp as the fangs surrounding him on all sides.

Gasping for air, Moe "Snake-Eyes" Juarez fought to regain his composure after the harrowing near-strangulation at the

hands of El Frío's bodyguards. His eyes
burned and throat felt savagely
constricted, but he refused to let his
facade crack for even an instant.

All around him, the hardened White Fence
gang members watched the scene with a
mixture of predatory interest and casual
indifference. To these vicious
sociopaths, such flirtations with
violence were as natural as breathing.
They could switch from amiable
conversation to grisly torture on a dime
without batting an eye.

For a heart-stopping moment, Moe was
certain his impromptu "deep cover" hustle
was about to be terminally exposed as the
desperate con it was. Only El Frío's
fleeting amusement at the concept of
having a "Judas goat" from within Carmela
Delgado's ranks had spared him and
Freddie from immediate annihilation.

The PI's eyes flicked to his cowering companion, relieved to see the little safecracker was still breathing, however shallowly. Poor Freddie was clearly broken by their nightmarish descent into this urban hellscape. Moe wondered just how much longer the man's fragile psyche could endure before shattering completely.

His own resilience, however, was born from decades of walking the razor's edge between civility and brutality on East LA's streets. Despite the very real threat of an agonizing demise constantly looming, Moe felt an odd sense of comfort return to him in these squalid, violence-soaked environs. This was the world he knew, the rules he'd mastered from boyhood.

As El Frío continued holding court, Moe allowed his gaze to drift in an approximation of boredom and

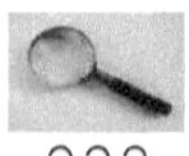

indifference. The vicious gang leader clearly relished imparting his sadistic ramblings to a "captive" audience, real or imagined. For now, Juarez's insane bluff was passing muster - but for how much longer?

It was then that his sharp eyes caught that glint again, unmistakable even in the hazy light. There, on the slim wrist of the diminutive crime boss amid the garish tatted sleeves and obscene gold jewelry, a distinctive and clearly antiqued timepiece peeked forth.

A true aficionado's collector's item, that much was obvious even from a cursory glance. The sort of watch only the most dedicated and wealthy enthusiasts could ever dream of possessing. What unfathomable acts of depravity had El Frío committed to claim such a sinister trophy?

Moe's instincts began tingling almost subliminally...was there an even more insidious tale behind that unassuming wristwatch nestled amidst the White Fence trappings of gang culture? A lead, a thread, a tantalizing opportunity to potentially turn the entire tables if he could just keep his wits about him in this rapidly-shifting house of sadistic violence?

His eyes must have betrayed too keen an interest, for suddenly El Frío's mocking diatribe ceased. Those pitiless obsidian orbs locked dead on Moe, studying him with the intensity of a coiled snake assessing a potentially-lethal threat.

"Perhaps you have question about the luxuries one can enjoy through complete ponder on these streets?"

Moe felt a bead of sweat trickle down the nape of his neck, but otherwise kept his

stance relaxed, open. Deflecting or backpedaling now could prove disastrous.

"I just appreciate the eccentricities in life, I guess you could say," he replied slowly, holding El Frío's gaze steadily. "Never figured a hard case like yourself for having much interest for collecting little pretties like that."

A silence fell over the room as the gathered White Fence hardcases sized up the PI with a mixture of open scorn and wariness. Finally, their diminutive leader let a thin smile of amusement curl across his features.

"You would be surprised how sentimental one can become over such exquisite decorations, detective. Even those of us who have long abandoned any moral compunctions we still occasionally indulge in nostalgia."

My Other Works Include:

The Robin Hood Virus

The Robin Hood Virus - Discovery

The Robin Hood Virus - Validation

Worldwide Trivia from the 1930's including Military Trivia Book 1

Worldwide Trivia from the 1930's including Military Trivia Book 2

Worldwide Trivia from the 1930's including Military Trivia Book 3

A Riverboat Odyssey

A Riverboat Odyssey - Astrid's Final Journey

Turbo - A Private Detective in East Los
Angeles during the 1960's

Turbo - A Private Detective in East Los
Angeles during the 1970's